WILLIAM SHAKESPEARE

The MERCHANT of VENICE

CAMPFIRE™

KALYANI NAVYUG MEDIA PVT. LTD.
New Delhi

The MERCHANT of VENICE

Sitting around the Campfire, telling the story, were:

WORDSMITH JOHN F. MCDONALD
ILLUSTRATOR VINOD KUMAR
COLORIST ANIL C. K.
LETTERER LAXMI CHAND GUPTA
EDITORS DIVYA DUBEY & ANDREW DODD
EDITOR (INFORMATIVE CONTENT) RASHMI MENON
PRODUCTION CONTROLLER VISHAL SHARMA
ART DIRECTOR RAJESH NAGULAKONDA
COVER ART VINOD KUMAR & JAYAKRISHNAN K. P.
DESIGNER JAYAKRISHNAN K. P.

CAMPFIRE™

www.campfire.co.in

Published by Kalyani Navyug Media Pvt. Ltd.

101 C, Shiv House, Hari Nagar Ashram, New Delhi 110014 India

ISBN: 978-93-80028-59-0

Printed in India at Rave India

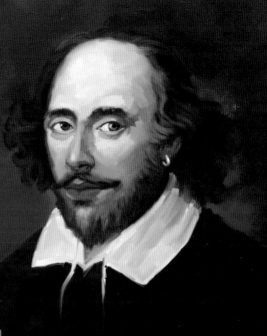

ABOUT THE AUTHOR

Famously known as 'The Bard of Avon', William Shakespeare was born in Stratford-upon-Avon, most probably on April 23, 1564. We say probably because till date, nobody has conclusive evidence for Shakespeare's birthday.

His father, John Shakespeare, was a successful local businessman and his mother, Mary Arden, was the daughter of a wealthy landowner. In 1582, an eighteen-year-old William married an older woman named Anne Hathaway. Soon, they had their first daughter, Susanna and later, another two children. William's only son, Hamnet, died at the tender age of eleven.

Translated into innumerable languages across the globe, Shakespeare's plays and sonnets are undoubtedly the most studied writings in the English language. A rare playwright, he excelled in tragedies, comedies, and histories. Skillfully combining entertainment with unmatched poetry, some of his most famous plays are *Othello, Macbeth, A Midsummer Night's Dream, Romeo and Juliet,* and *The Merchant of Venice,* among many others.

Shakespeare was also an actor. In 1599, he became one of the partners in the new Globe Theatre in London and a part owner of his own theater company called 'The Chamberlain's Men'—a group of remarkable actors who were also business partners and close friends of Shakespeare. When Queen Elizabeth died in 1603 and was succeeded by her cousin King James of Scotland, 'The Chamberlain's Men' was renamed 'The King's Men'.

Shakespeare died in 1616. It is not clear how he died, although his vicar suggested it was from heavy drinking.

The characters he created and the stories he told have held the interest of people for the past 400 years! Till date, his plays are performed all over the world and have been turned into movies, comics, cartoons, operas, and musicals.

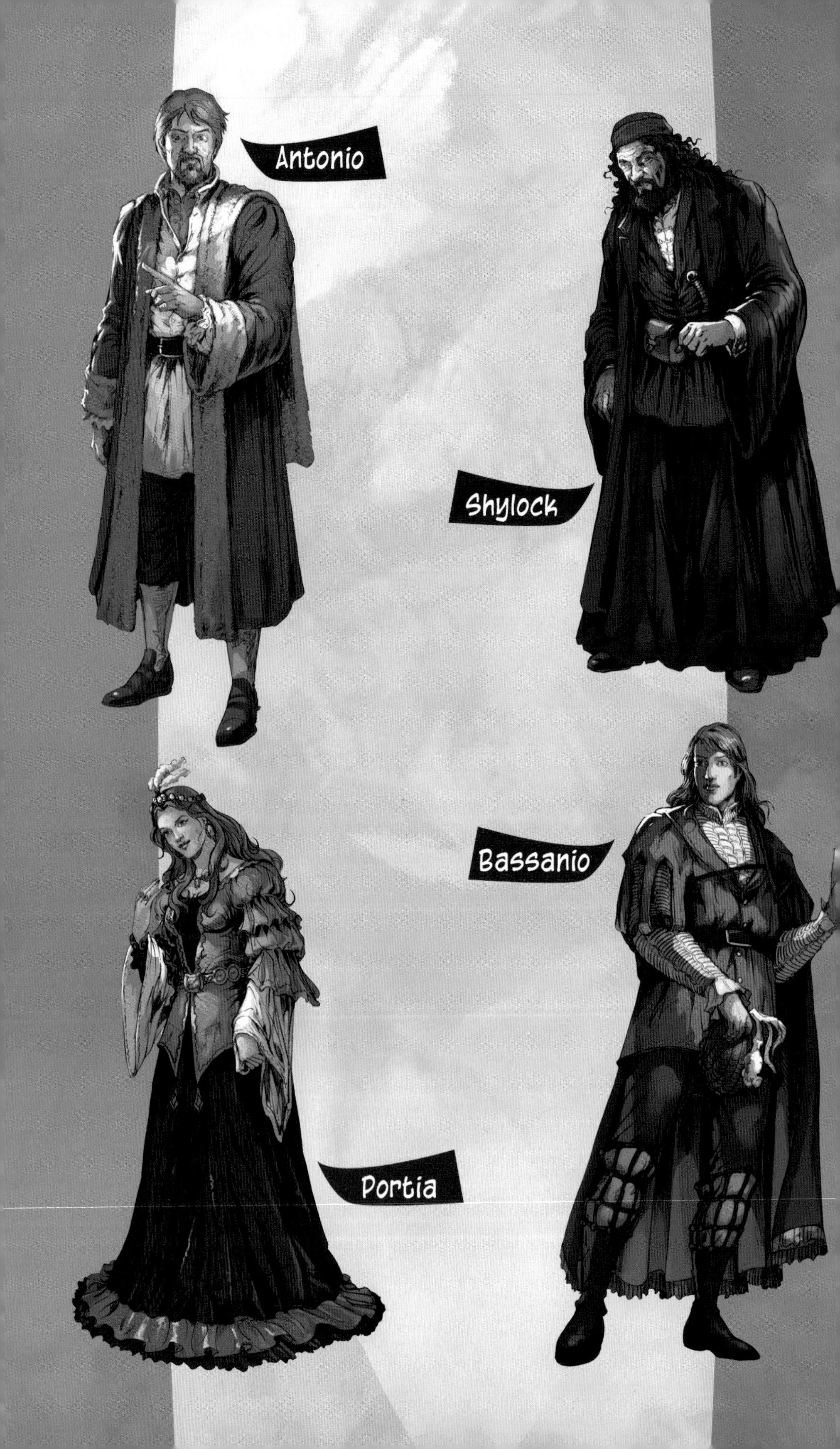
Antonio
Shylock
Bassanio
Portia

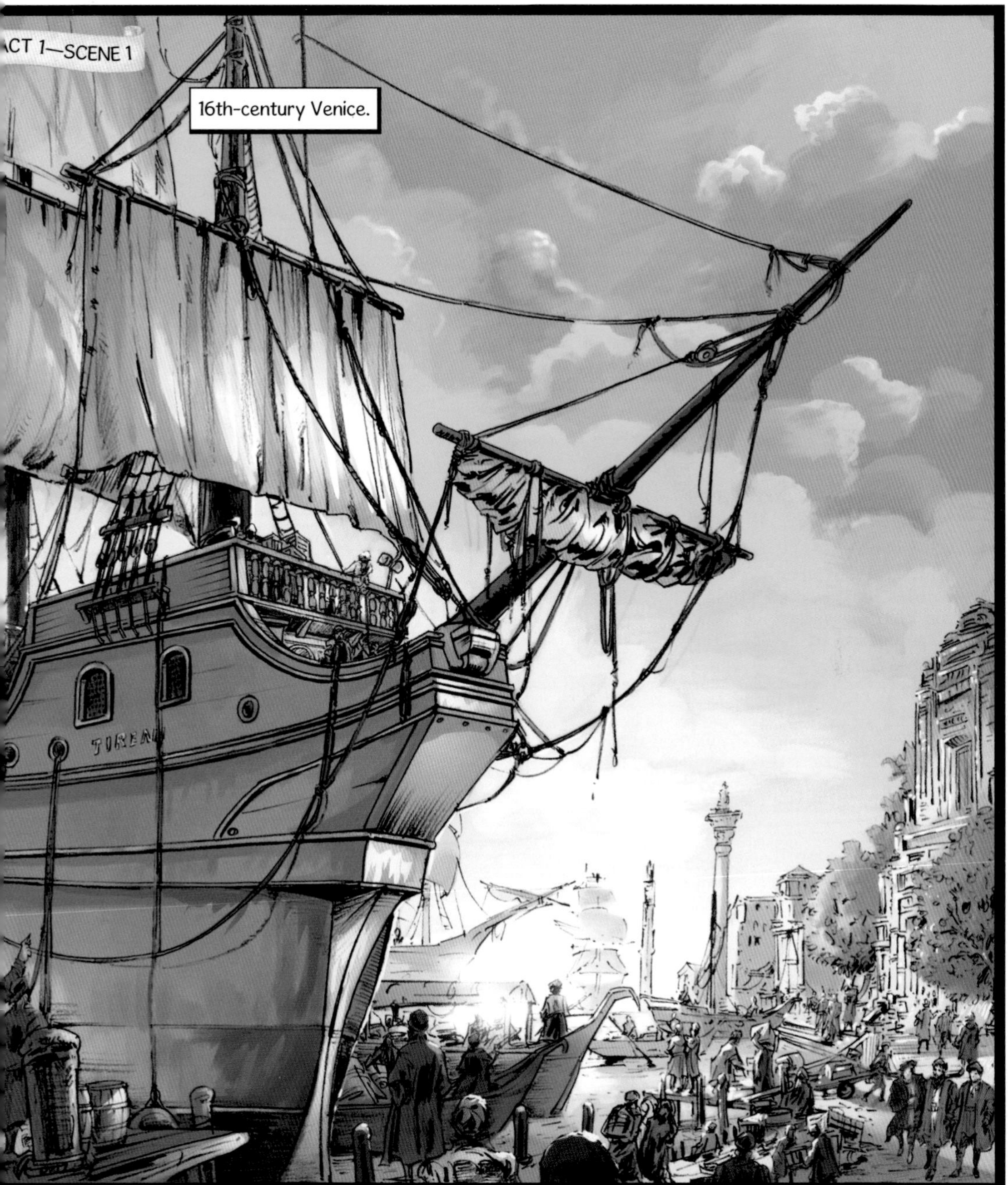
ACT 1—SCENE 1
16th-century Venice.

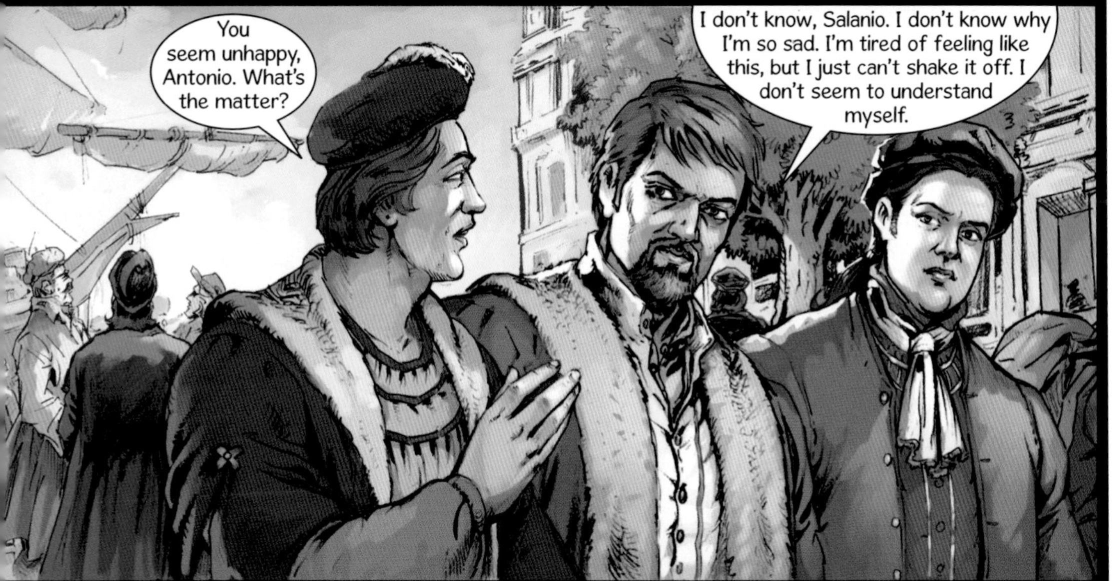
You seem unhappy, Antonio. What's the matter?
I don't know, Salanio. I don't know why I'm so sad. I'm tired of feeling like this, but I just can't shake it off. I don't seem to understand myself.

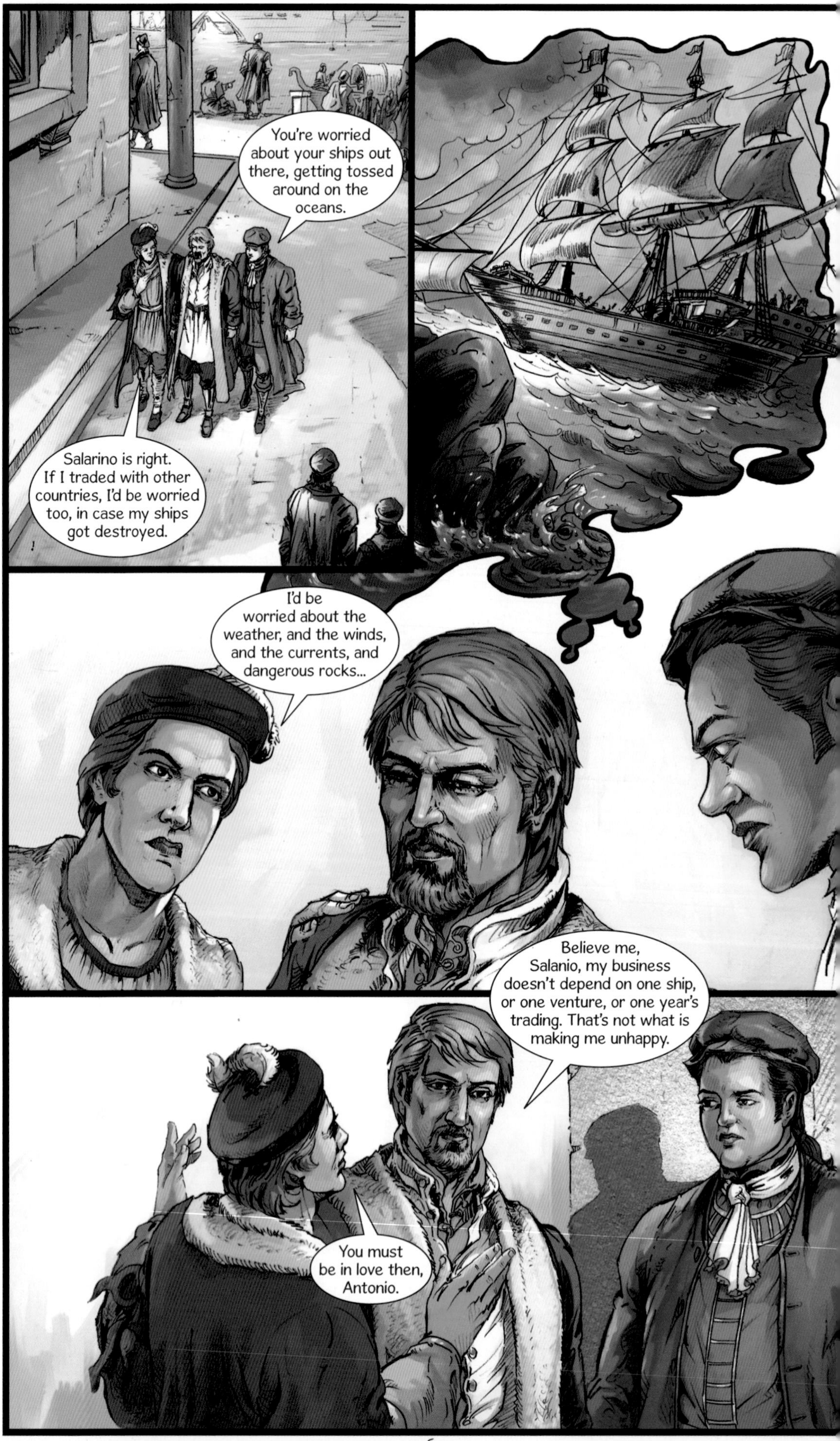
You're worried about your ships out there, getting tossed around on the oceans.
Salarino is right. If I traded with other countries, I'd be worried too, in case my ships got destroyed.
I'd be worried about the weather, and the winds, and the currents, and dangerous rocks...
Believe me, Salanio, my business doesn't depend on one ship, or one venture, or one year's trading. That's not what is making me unhappy.
You must be in love then, Antonio.

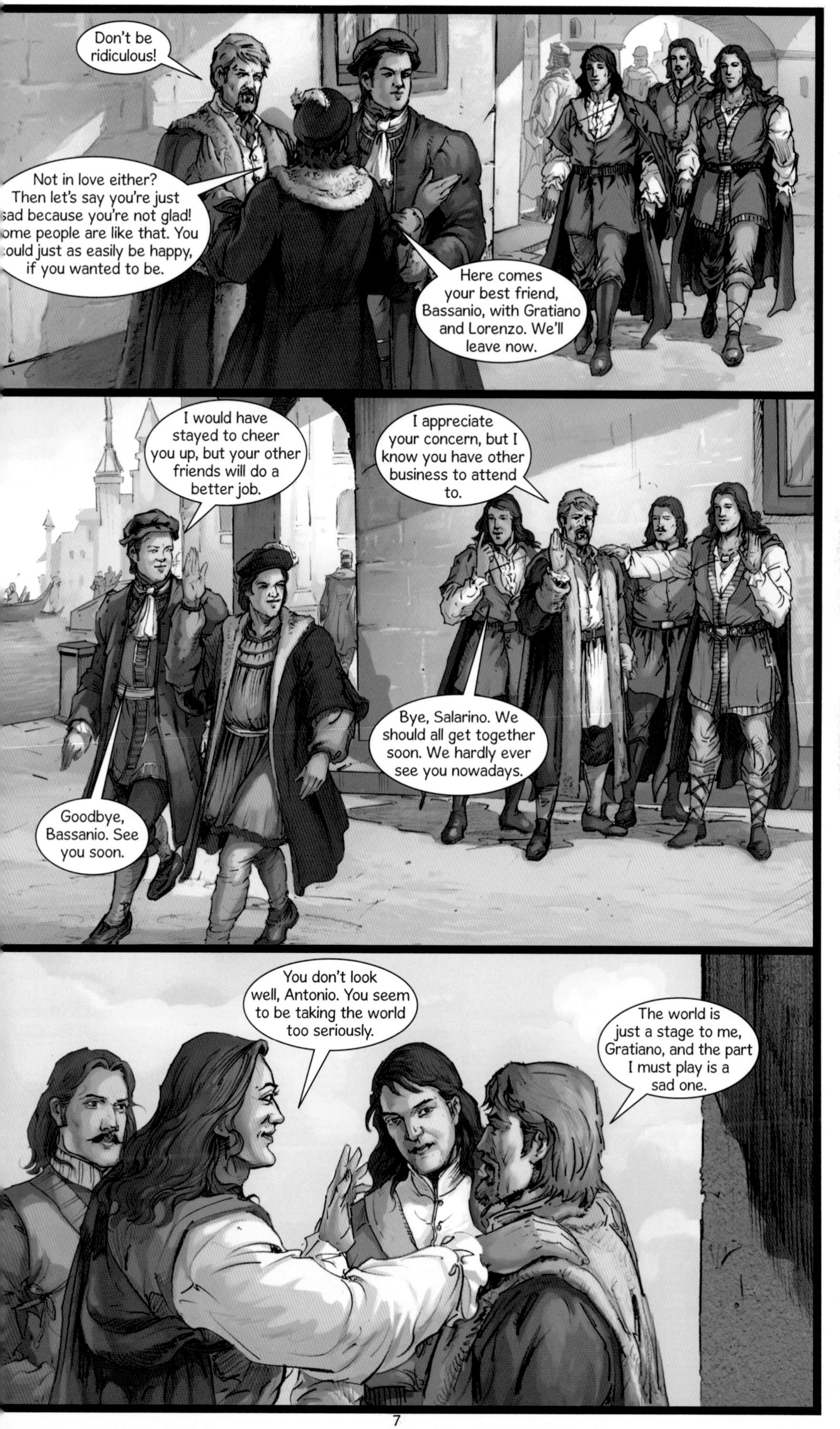
Don't be ridiculous!
Not in love either? Then let's say you're just sad because you're not glad! Some people are like that. You could just as easily be happy, if you wanted to be.
Here comes your best friend, Bassanio, with Gratiano and Lorenzo. We'll leave now.
I would have stayed to cheer you up, but your other friends will do a better job.
I appreciate your concern, but I know you have other business to attend to.
Bye, Salarino. We should all get together soon. We hardly ever see you nowadays.
Goodbye, Bassanio. See you soon.
You don't look well, Antonio. You seem to be taking the world too seriously.
The world is just a stage to me, Gratiano, and the part I must play is a sad one.

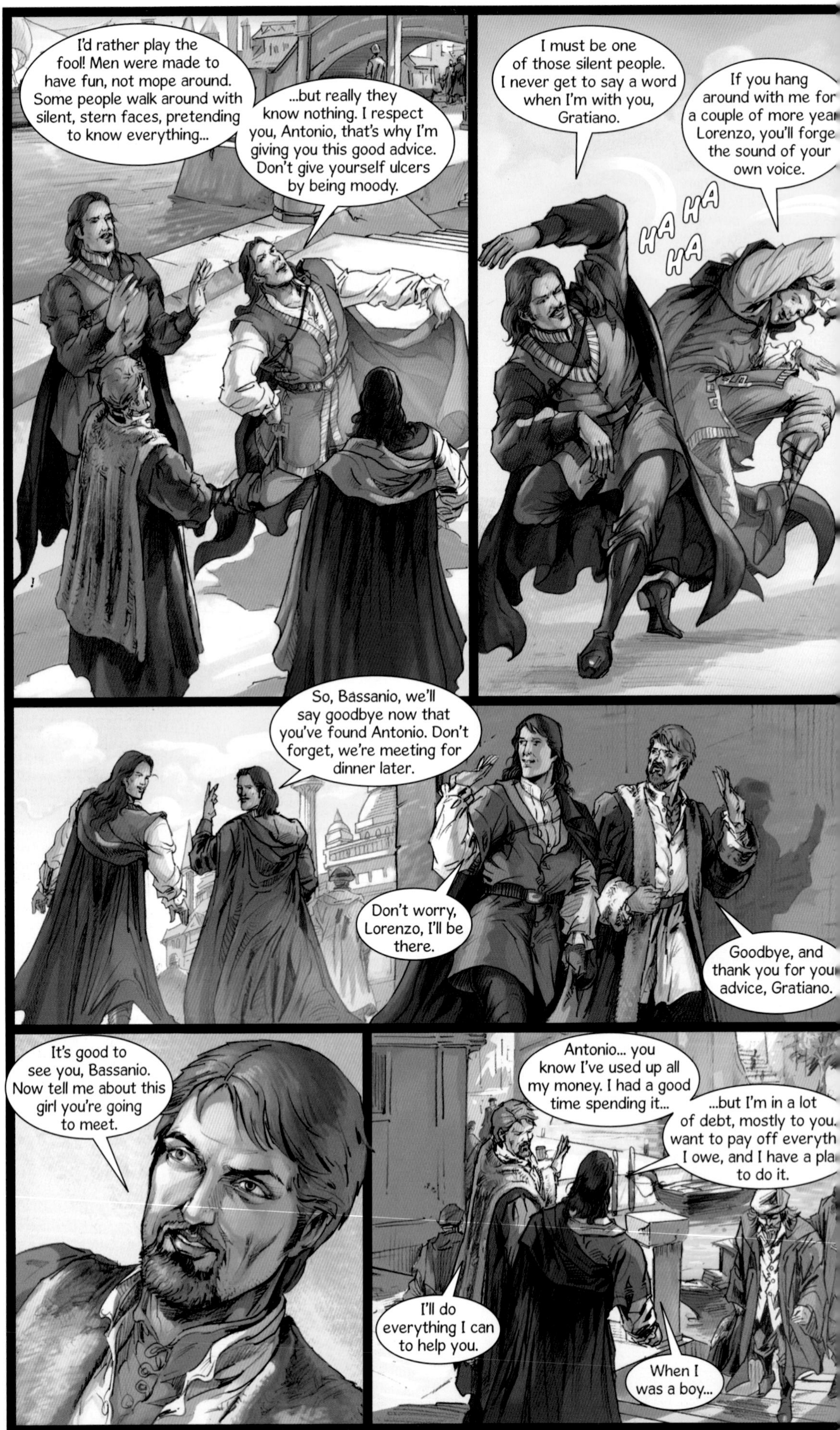

I'd rather play the fool! Men were made to have fun, not mope around. Some people walk around with silent, stern faces, pretending to know everything...
...but really they know nothing. I respect you, Antonio, that's why I'm giving you this good advice. Don't give yourself ulcers by being moody.
I must be one of those silent people. I never get to say a word when I'm with you, Gratiano.
If you hang around with me for a couple of more yea Lorenzo, you'll forge the sound of your own voice.
HA HA HA
So, Bassanio, we'll say goodbye now that you've found Antonio. Don't forget, we're meeting for dinner later.
Don't worry, Lorenzo, I'll be there.
Goodbye, and thank you for you advice, Gratiano.
It's good to see you, Bassanio. Now tell me about this girl you're going to meet.
Antonio... you know I've used up all my money. I had a good time spending it...
...but I'm in a lot of debt, mostly to you. want to pay off everyth I owe, and I have a pla to do it.
I'll do everything I can to help you.
When I was a boy...

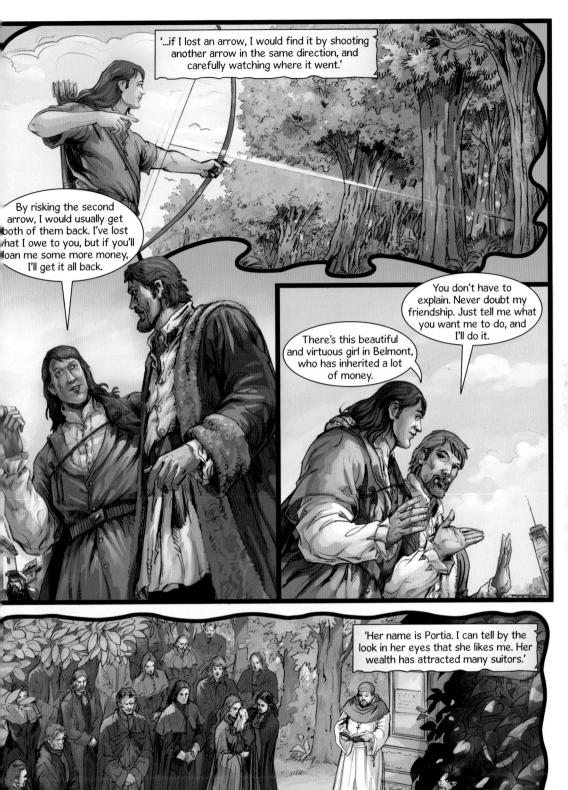

'...if I lost an arrow, I would find it by shooting another arrow in the same direction, and carefully watching where it went.'

By risking the second arrow, I would usually get both of them back. I've lost what I owe to you, but if you'll loan me some more money, I'll get it all back.

You don't have to explain. Never doubt my friendship. Just tell me what you want me to do, and I'll do it.

There's this beautiful and virtuous girl in Belmont, who has inherited a lot of money.

'Her name is Portia. I can tell by the look in her eyes that she likes me. Her wealth has attracted many suitors.'

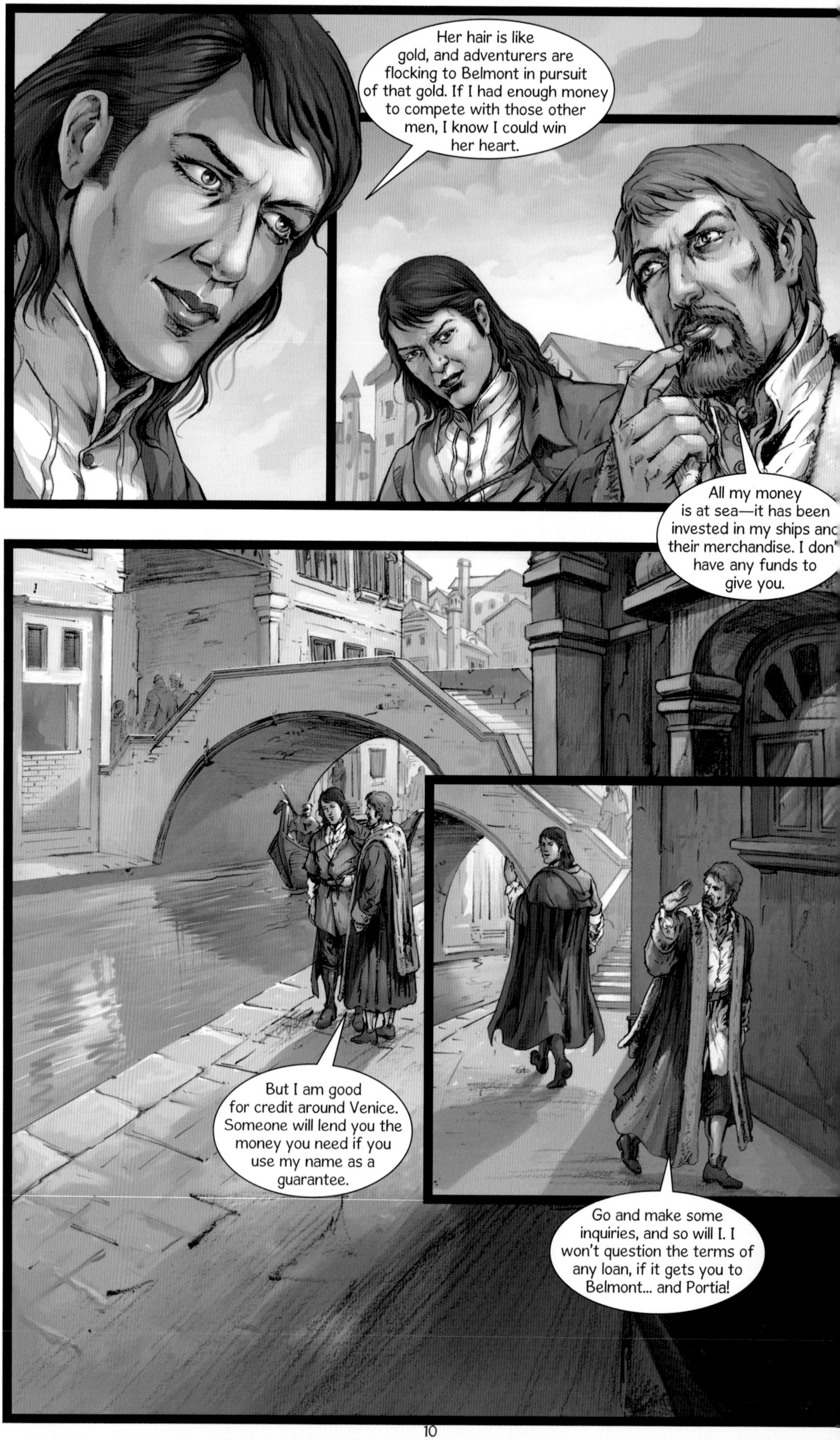

Her hair is like gold, and adventurers are flocking to Belmont in pursuit of that gold. If I had enough money to compete with those other men, I know I could win her heart.
All my money is at sea—it has been invested in my ships and their merchandise. I don't have any funds to give you.
But I am good for credit around Venice. Someone will lend you the money you need if you use my name as a guarantee.
Go and make some inquiries, and so will I. I won't question the terms of any loan, if it gets you to Belmont... and Portia!

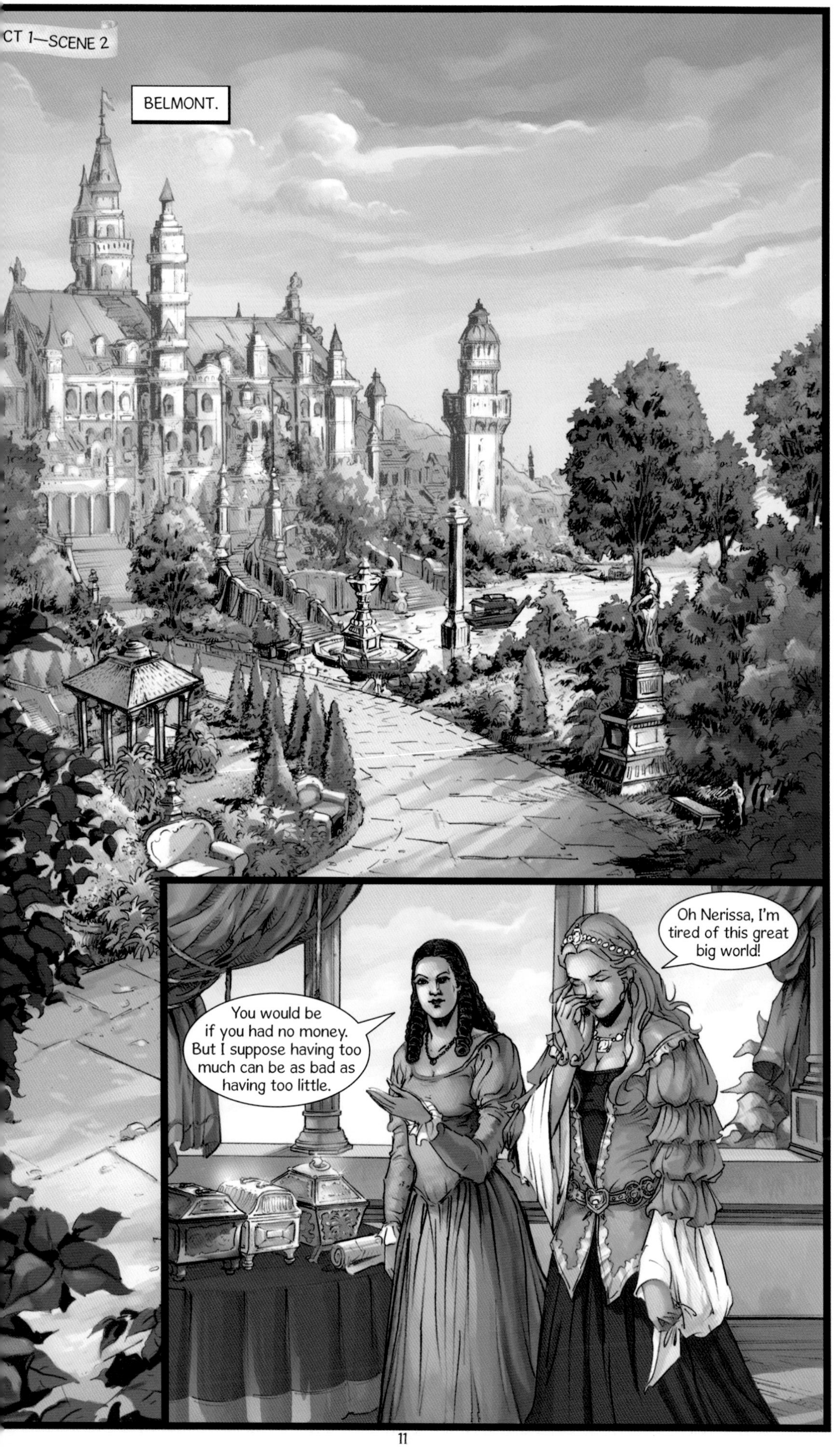
CT 1—SCENE 2
BELMONT.
Oh Nerissa, I'm tired of this great big world!
You would be if you had no money. But I suppose having too much can be as bad as having too little.

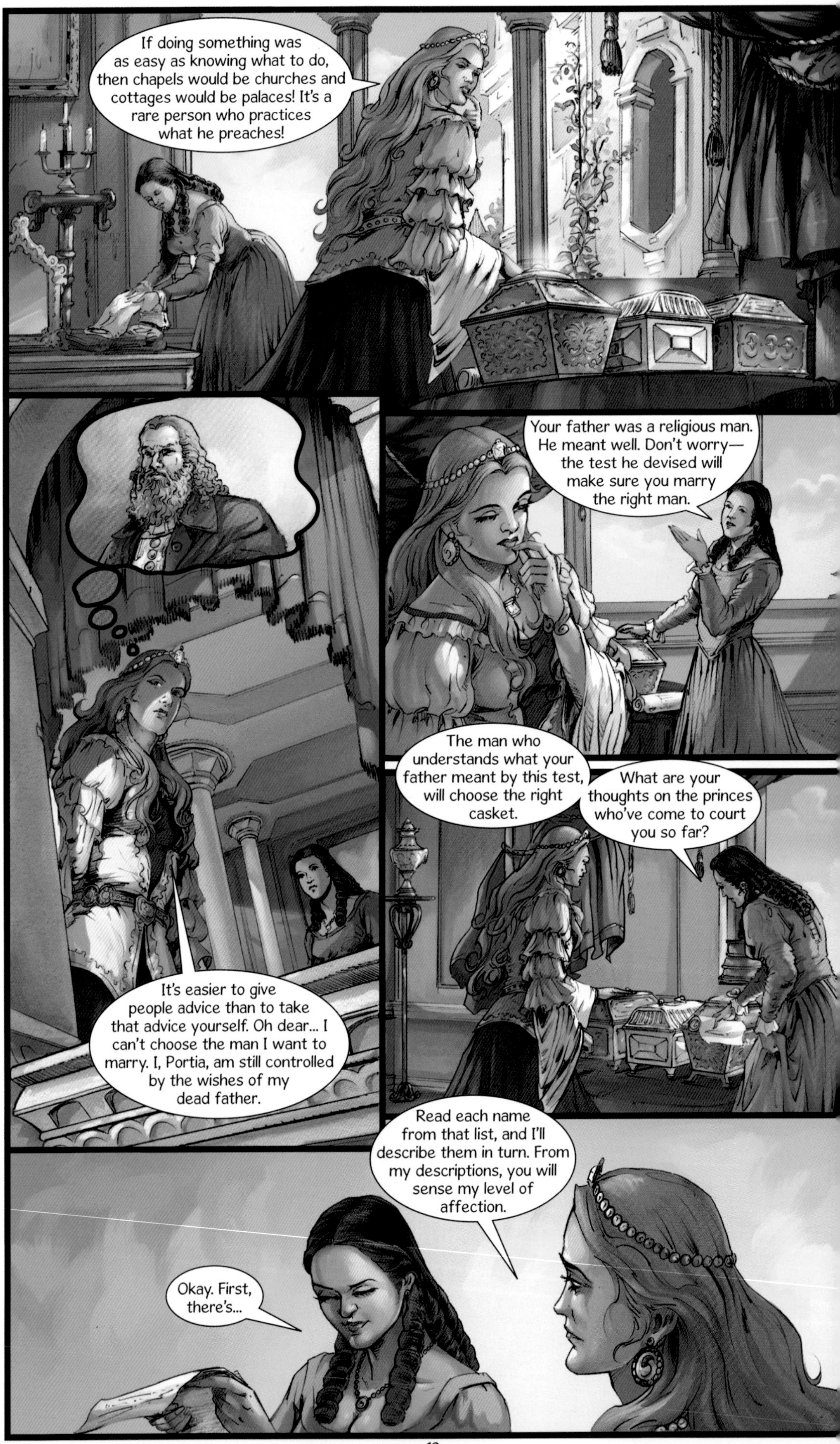
If doing something was as easy as knowing what to do, then chapels would be churches and cottages would be palaces! It's a rare person who practices what he preaches!
It's easier to give people advice than to take that advice yourself. Oh dear... I can't choose the man I want to marry. I, Portia, am still controlled by the wishes of my dead father.
Your father was a religious man. He meant well. Don't worry—the test he devised will make sure you marry the right man.
The man who understands what your father meant by this test, will choose the right casket.
What are your thoughts on the princes who've come to court you so far?
Read each name from that list, and I'll describe them in turn. From my descriptions, you will sense my level of affection.
Okay. First, there's...

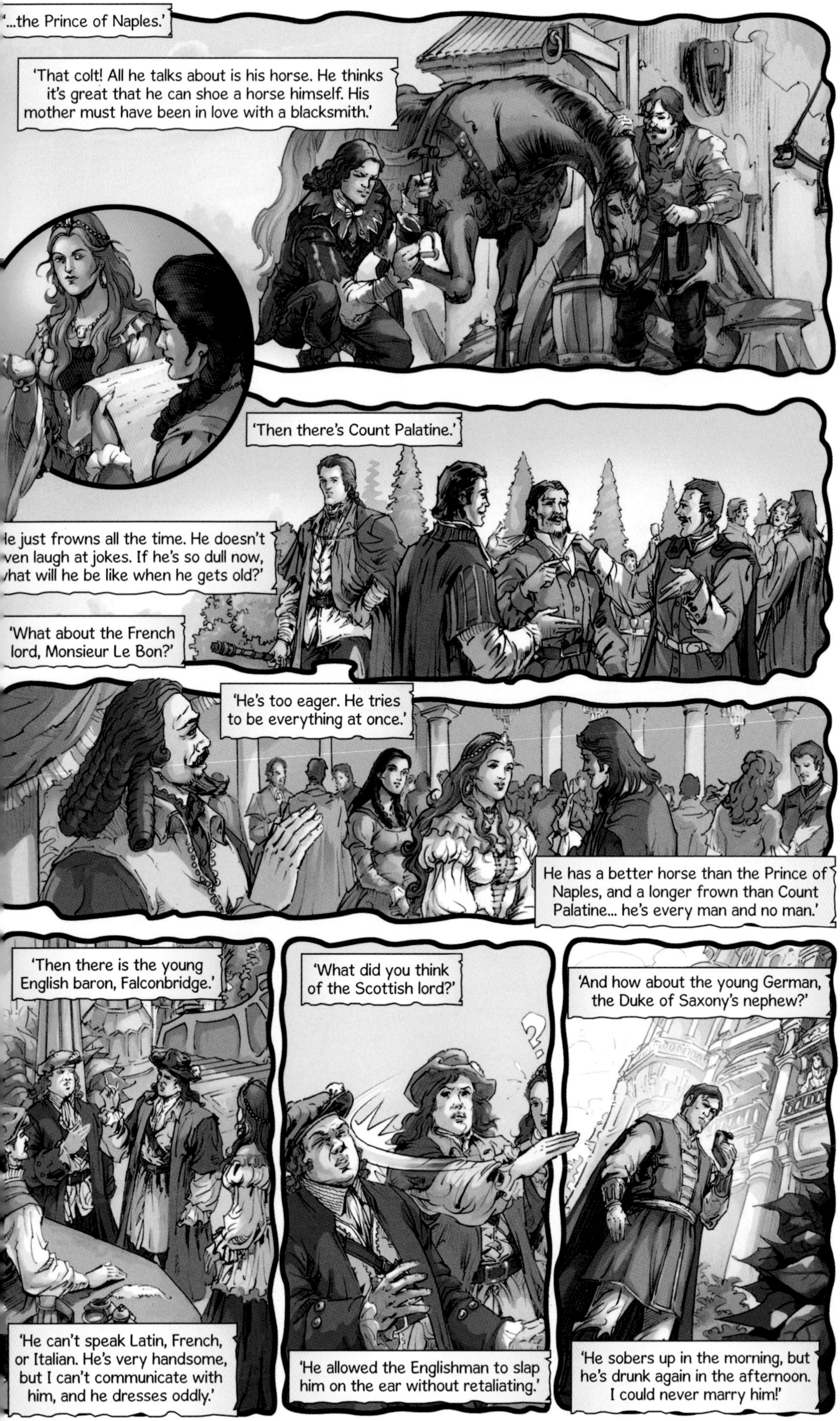
'...the Prince of Naples.'
'That colt! All he talks about is his horse. He thinks it's great that he can shoe a horse himself. His mother must have been in love with a blacksmith.'
'Then there's Count Palatine.'
le just frowns all the time. He doesn't ven laugh at jokes. If he's so dull now, hat will he be like when he gets old?'
'What about the French lord, Monsieur Le Bon?'
'He's too eager. He tries to be everything at once.'
He has a better horse than the Prince of Naples, and a longer frown than Count Palatine... he's every man and no man.'
'Then there is the young English baron, Falconbridge.'
'He can't speak Latin, French, or Italian. He's very handsome, but I can't communicate with him, and he dresses oddly.'
'What did you think of the Scottish lord?'
'He allowed the Englishman to slap him on the ear without retaliating.'
'And how about the young German, the Duke of Saxony's nephew?'
'He sobers up in the morning, but he's drunk again in the afternoon. I could never marry him!'

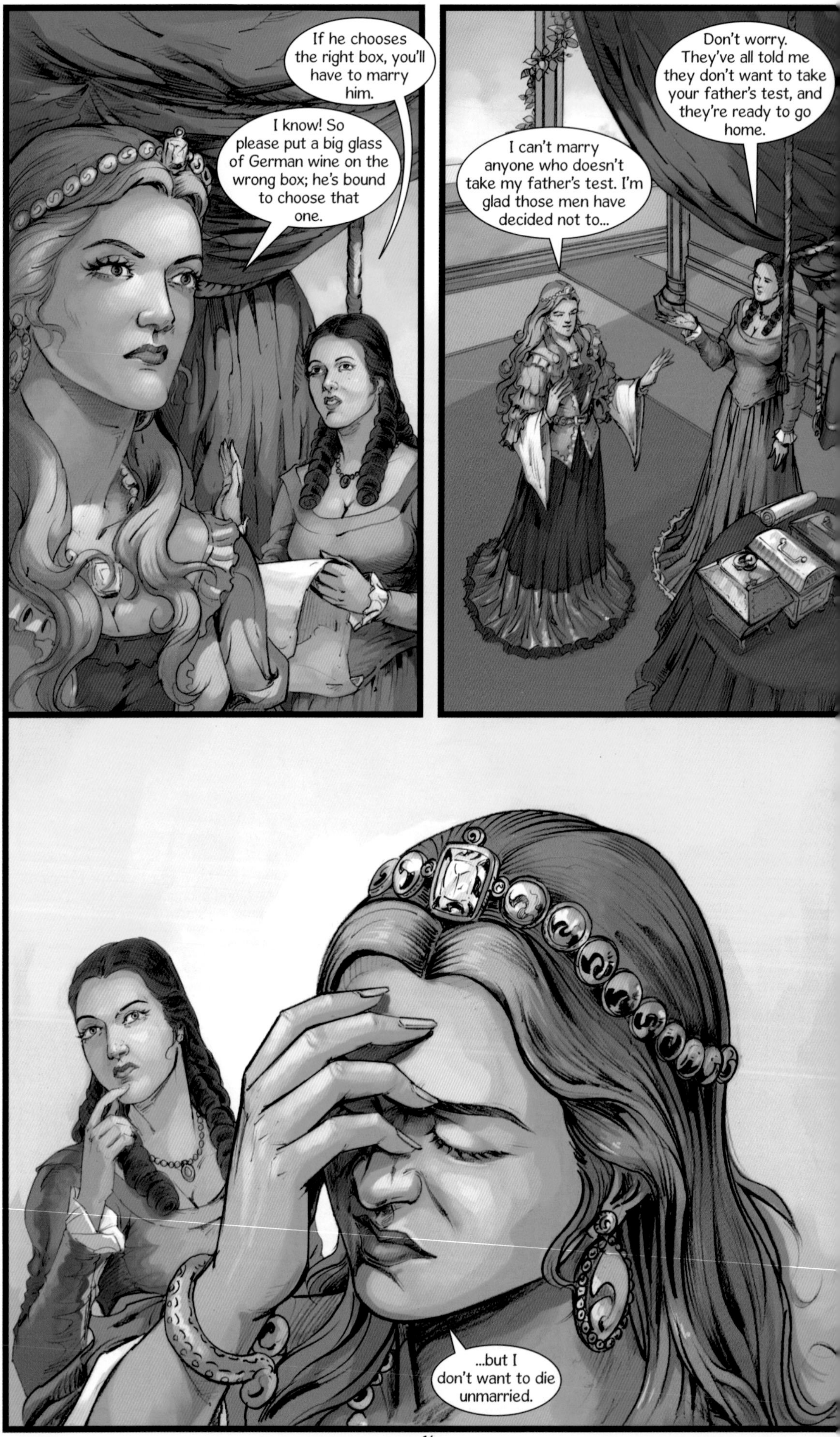

If he chooses the right box, you'll have to marry him.
I know! So please put a big glass of German wine on the wrong box; he's bound to choose that one.
Don't worry. They've all told me they don't want to take your father's test, and they're ready to go home.
I can't marry anyone who doesn't take my father's test. I'm glad those men have decided not to...
...but I don't want to die unmarried.

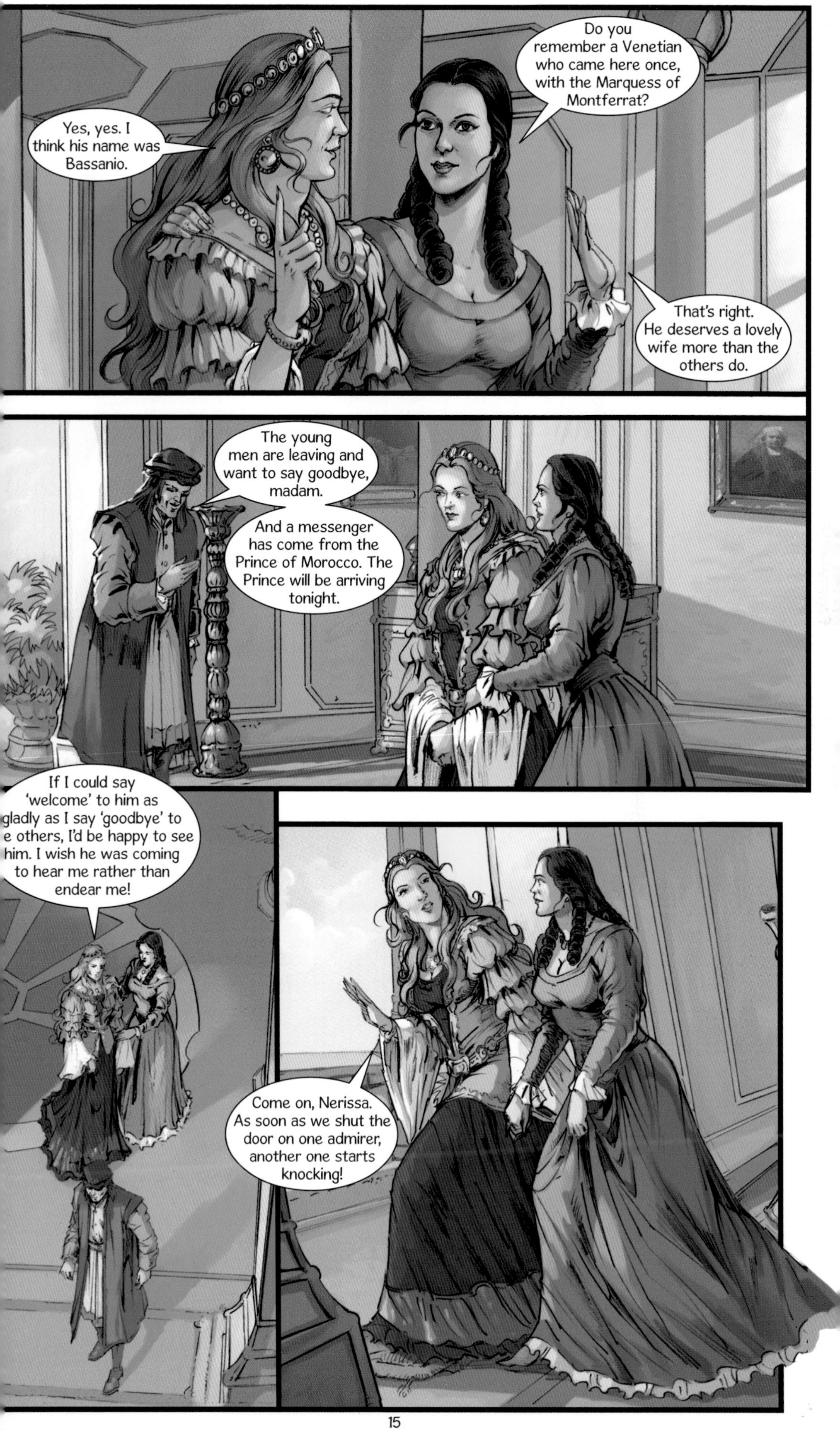
Do you remember a Venetian who came here once, with the Marquess of Montferrat?
Yes, yes. I think his name was Bassanio.
That's right. He deserves a lovely wife more than the others do.
The young men are leaving and want to say goodbye, madam.
And a messenger has come from the Prince of Morocco. The Prince will be arriving tonight.
If I could say 'welcome' to him as gladly as I say 'goodbye' to e others, I'd be happy to see him. I wish he was coming to hear me rather than endear me!
Come on, Nerissa. As soon as we shut the door on one admirer, another one starts knocking!

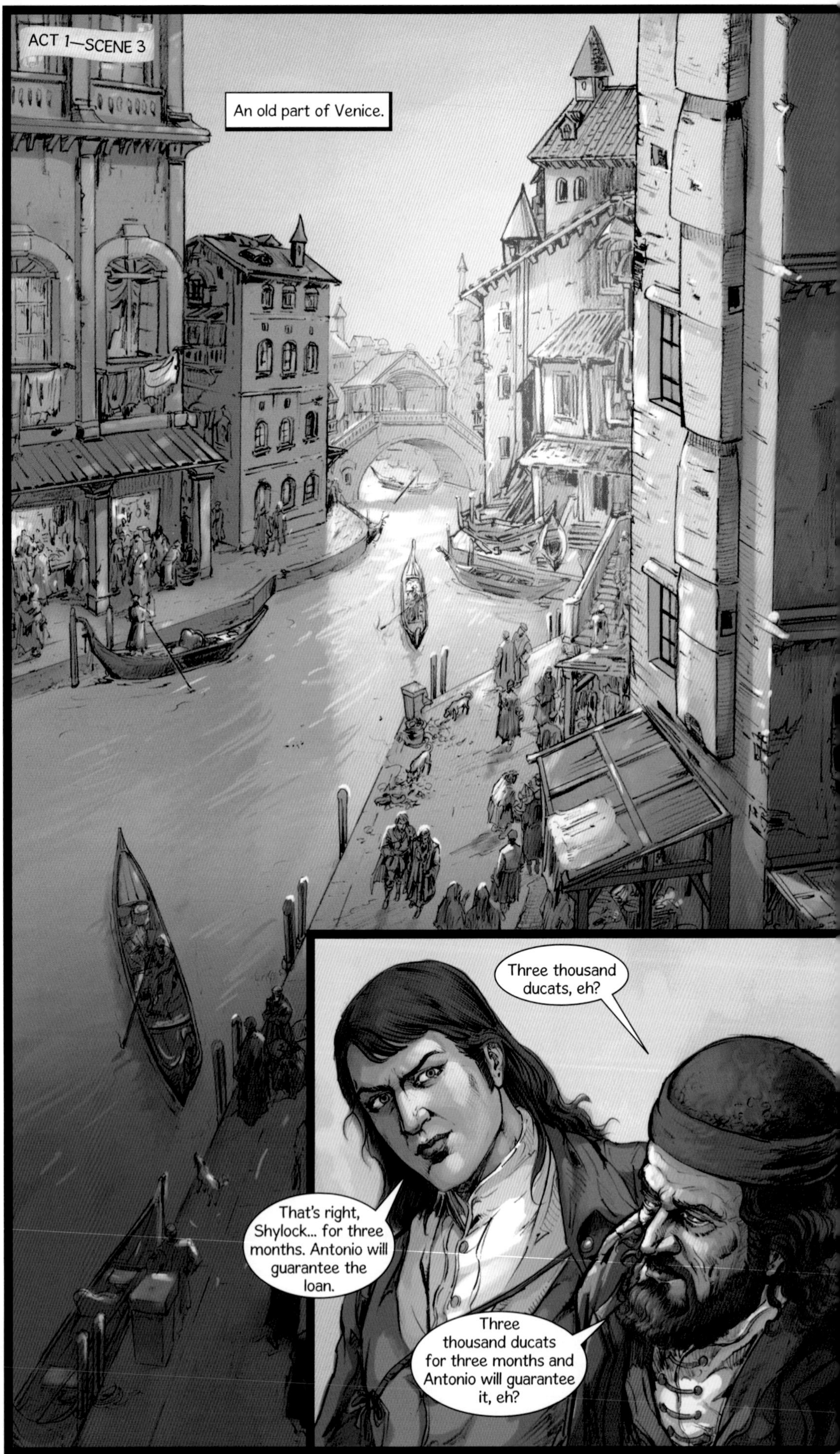
ACT 1—SCENE 3
An old part of Venice.
Three thousand ducats, eh?
That's right, Shylock... for three months. Antonio will guarantee the loan.
Three thousand ducats for three months and Antonio will guarantee it, eh?

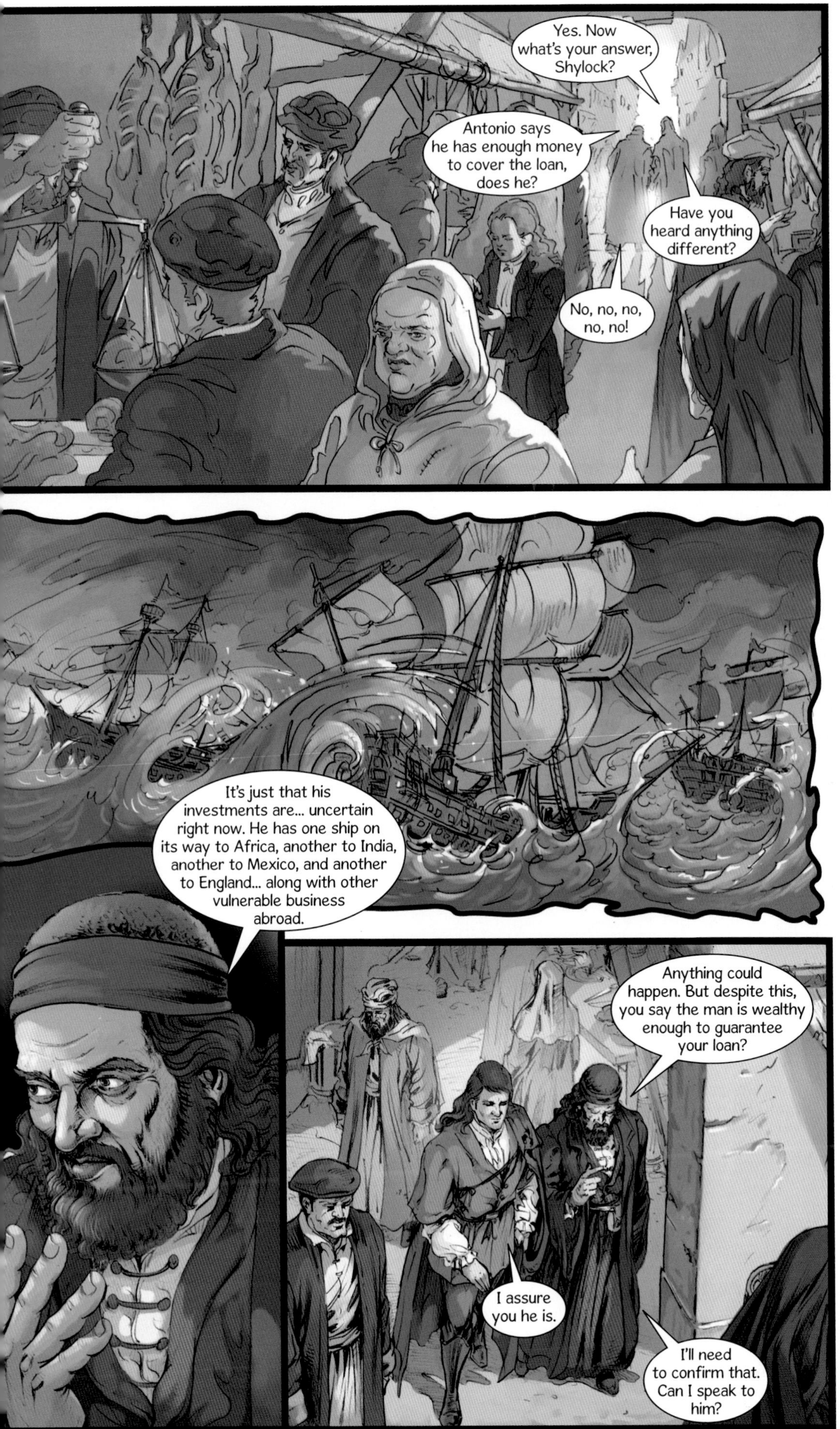
Yes. Now what's your answer, Shylock?
Antonio says he has enough money to cover the loan, does he?
Have you heard anything different?
No, no, no, no, no!
It's just that his investments are... uncertain right now. He has one ship on its way to Africa, another to India, another to Mexico, and another to England... along with other vulnerable business abroad.
Anything could happen. But despite this, you say the man is wealthy enough to guarantee your loan?
I assure you he is.
I'll need to confirm that. Can I speak to him?

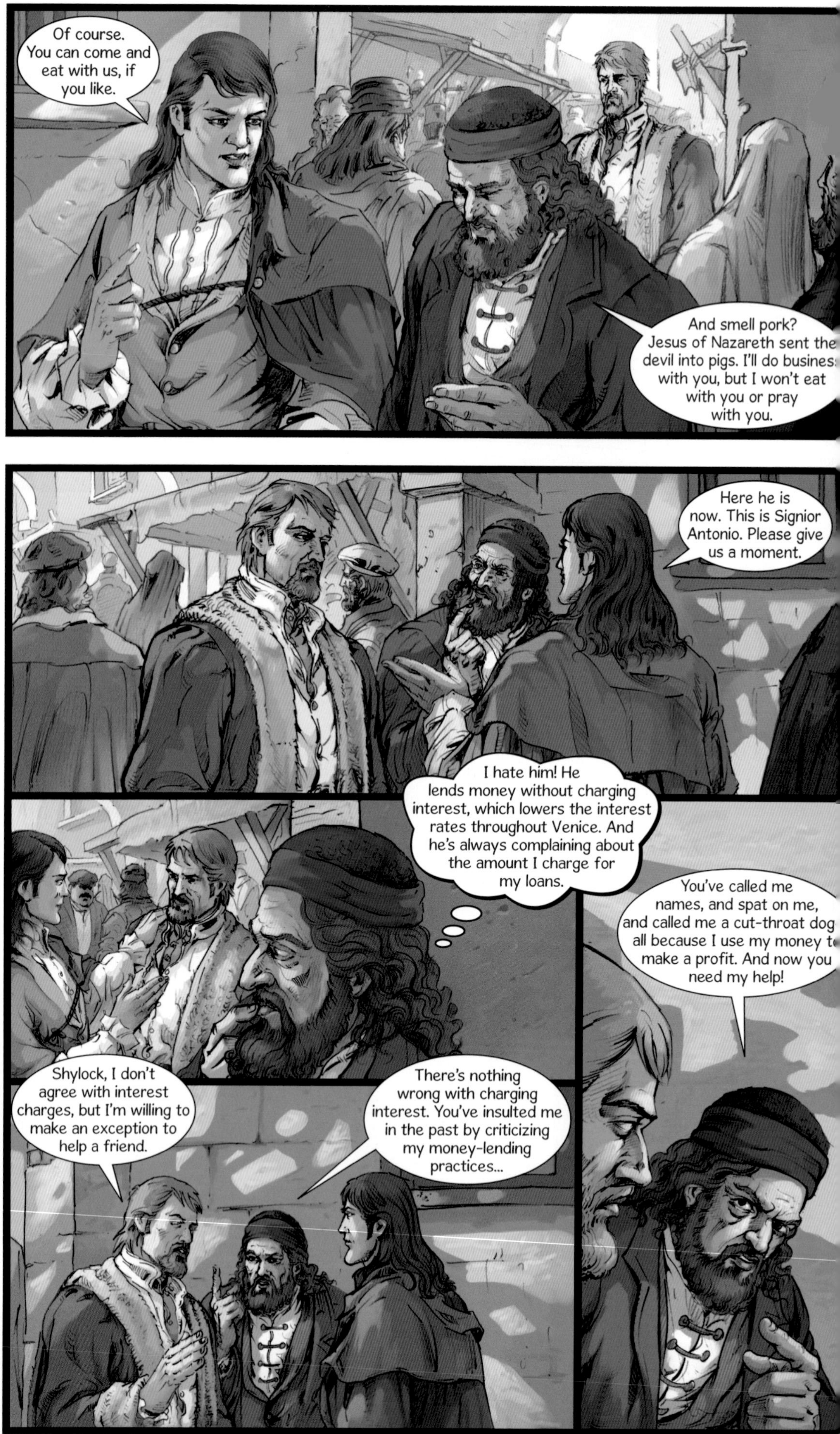
Of course. You can come and eat with us, if you like.
And smell pork? Jesus of Nazareth sent the devil into pigs. I'll do busines with you, but I won't eat with you or pray with you.
Here he is now. This is Signior Antonio. Please give us a moment.
I hate him! He lends money without charging interest, which lowers the interest rates throughout Venice. And he's always complaining about the amount I charge for my loans.
Shylock, I don't agree with interest charges, but I'm willing to make an exception to help a friend.
There's nothing wrong with charging interest. You've insulted me in the past by criticizing my money-lending practices...
You've called me names, and spat on me, and called me a cut-throat dog all because I use my money t make a profit. And now you need my help!

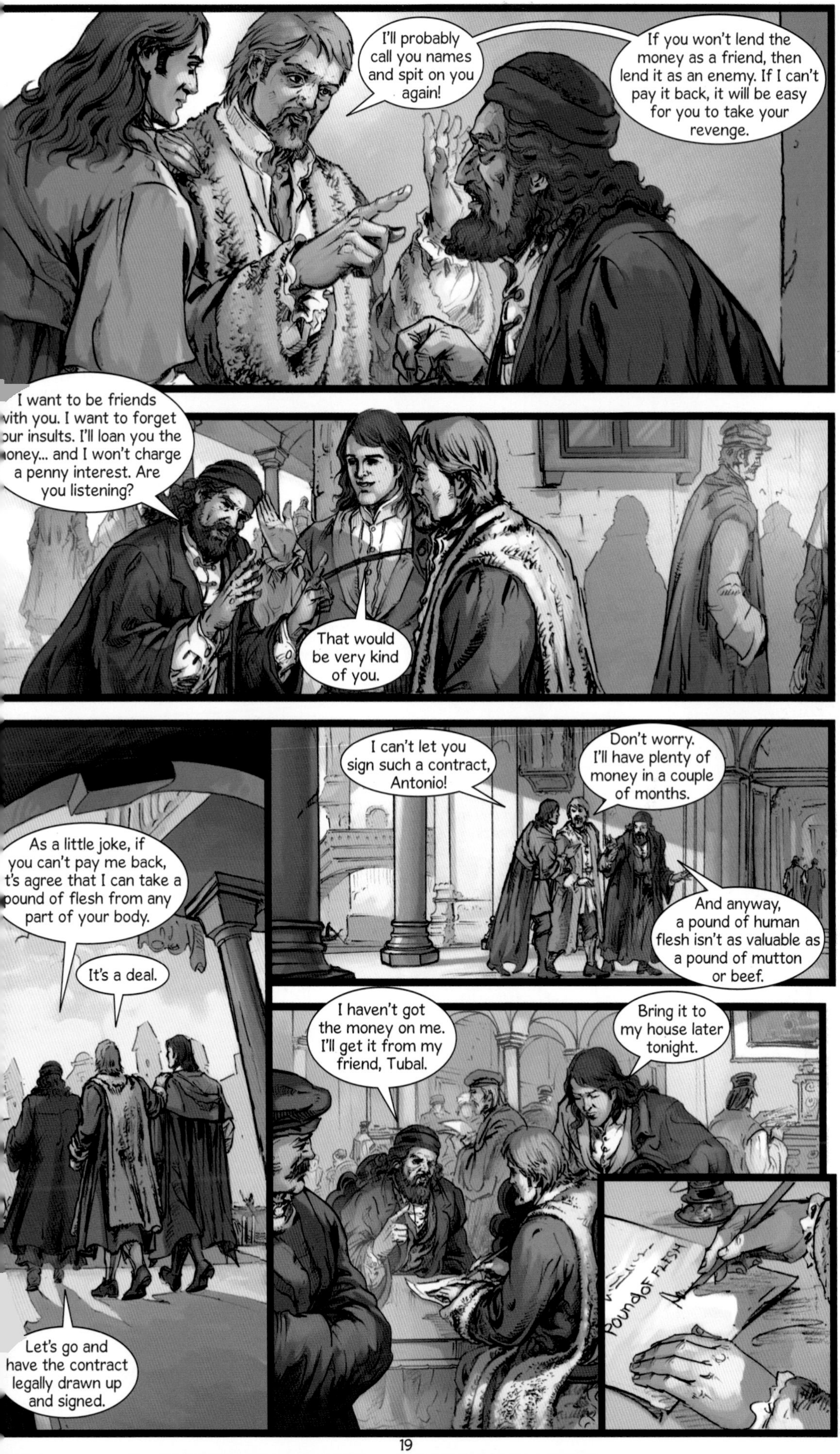
I'll probably call you names and spit on you again!
If you won't lend the money as a friend, then lend it as an enemy. If I can't pay it back, it will be easy for you to take your revenge.
I want to be friends with you. I want to forget our insults. I'll loan you the money... and I won't charge a penny interest. Are you listening?
That would be very kind of you.
As a little joke, if you can't pay me back, let's agree that I can take a pound of flesh from any part of your body.
It's a deal.
Let's go and have the contract legally drawn up and signed.
I can't let you sign such a contract, Antonio!
Don't worry. I'll have plenty of money in a couple of months.
And anyway, a pound of human flesh isn't as valuable as a pound of mutton or beef.
I haven't got the money on me. I'll get it from my friend, Tubal.
Bring it to my house later tonight.
POUND OF FLESH

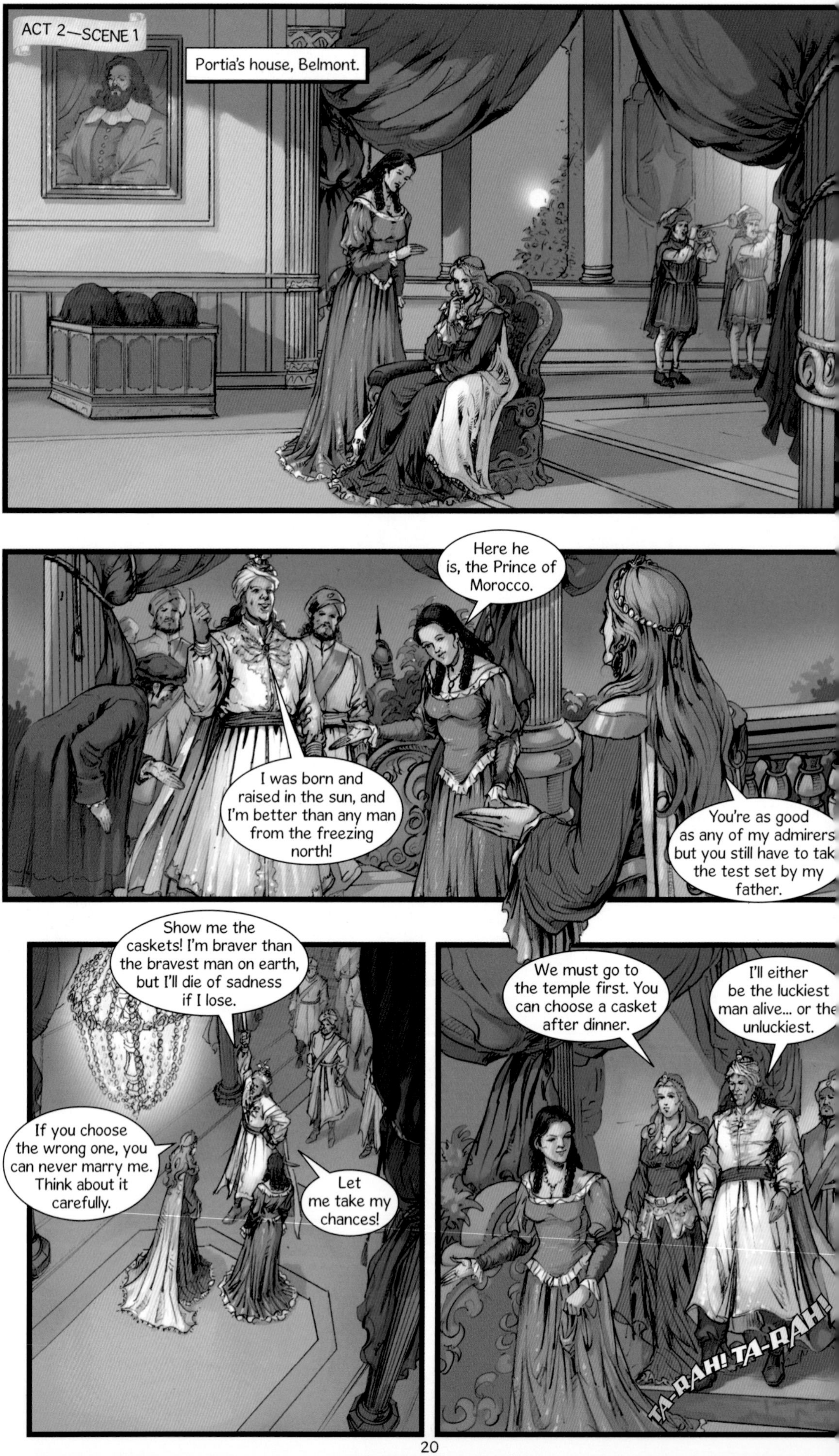
ACT 2—SCENE 1
Portia's house, Belmont.
Here he is, the Prince of Morocco.
I was born and raised in the sun, and I'm better than any man from the freezing north!
You're as good as any of my admirers but you still have to tak the test set by my father.
Show me the caskets! I'm braver than the bravest man on earth, but I'll die of sadness if I lose.
If you choose the wrong one, you can never marry me. Think about it carefully.
Let me take my chances!
We must go to the temple first. You can choose a casket after dinner.
I'll either be the luckiest man alive... or the unluckiest.
TA-RAH! TA-RAH!

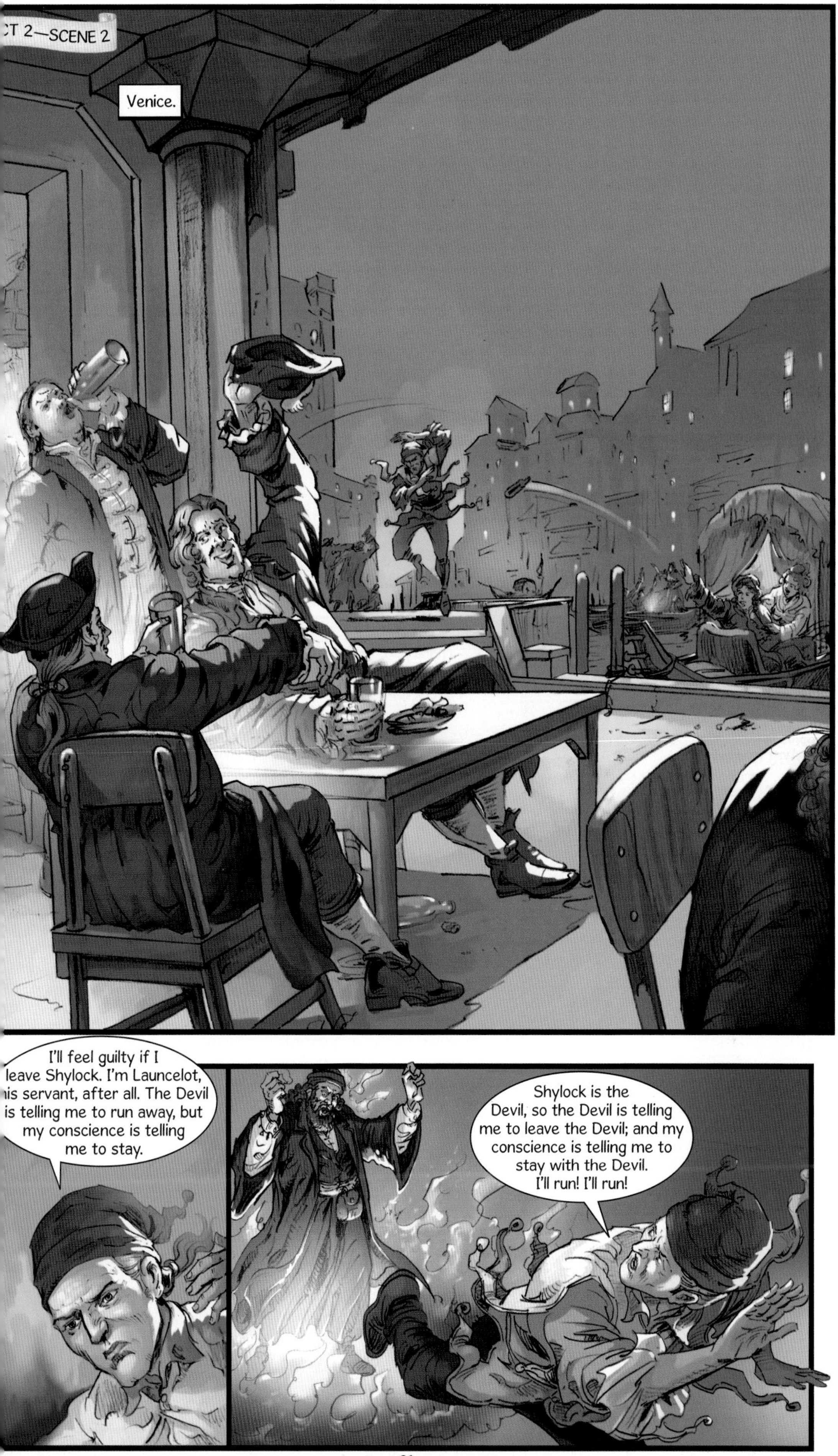
CT 2—SCENE 2
Venice.
I'll feel guilty if I leave Shylock. I'm Launcelot, is servant, after all. The Devil is telling me to run away, but my conscience is telling me to stay.
Shylock is the Devil, so the Devil is telling me to leave the Devil; and my conscience is telling me to stay with the Devil. I'll run! I'll run!

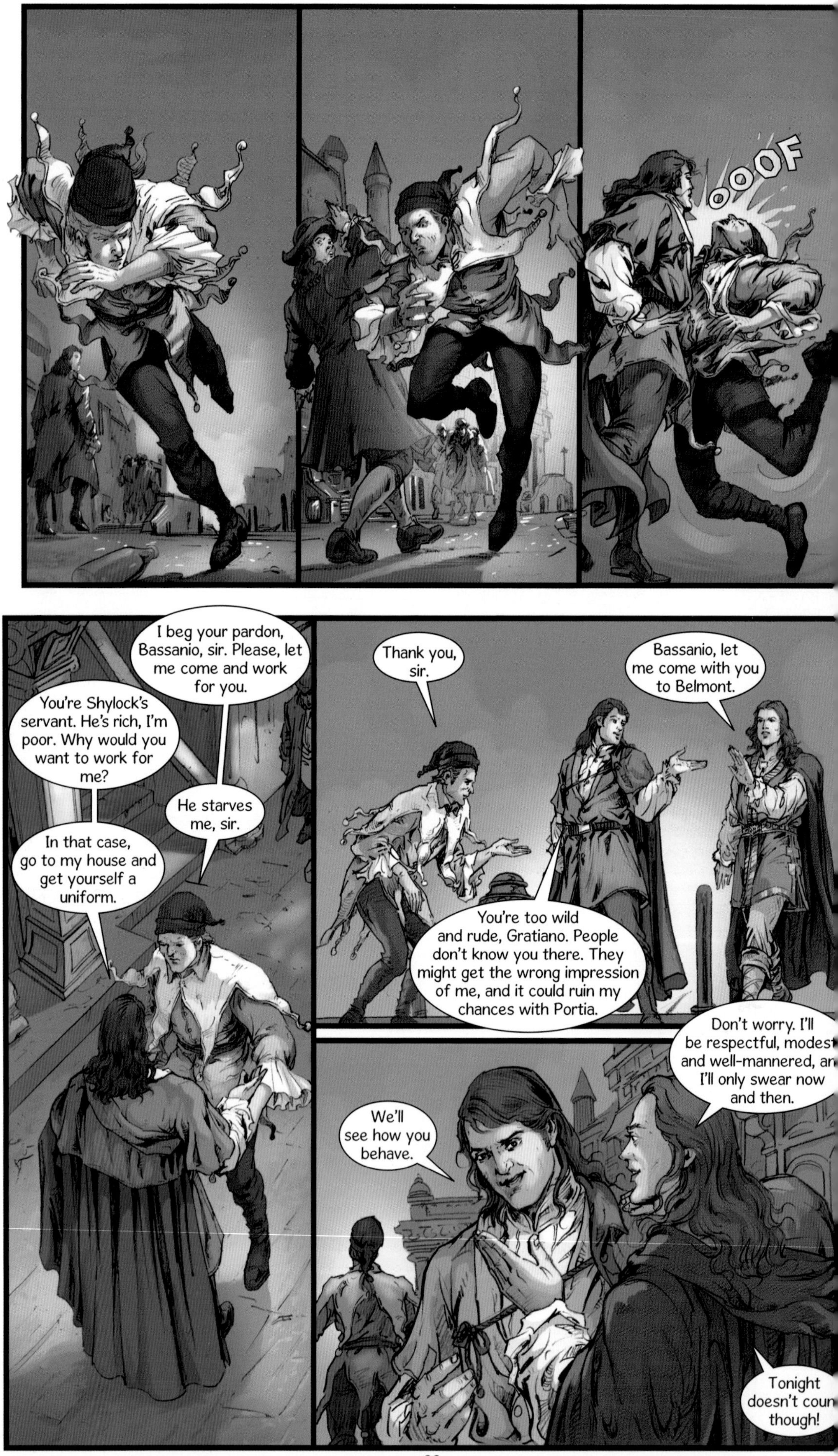
OOOF
I beg your pardon, Bassanio, sir. Please, let me come and work for you.
You're Shylock's servant. He's rich, I'm poor. Why would you want to work for me?
He starves me, sir.
In that case, go to my house and get yourself a uniform.
Thank you, sir.
Bassanio, let me come with you to Belmont.
You're too wild and rude, Gratiano. People don't know you there. They might get the wrong impression of me, and it could ruin my chances with Portia.
Don't worry. I'll be respectful, modes and well-mannered, an I'll only swear now and then.
We'll see how you behave.
Tonight doesn't coun though!

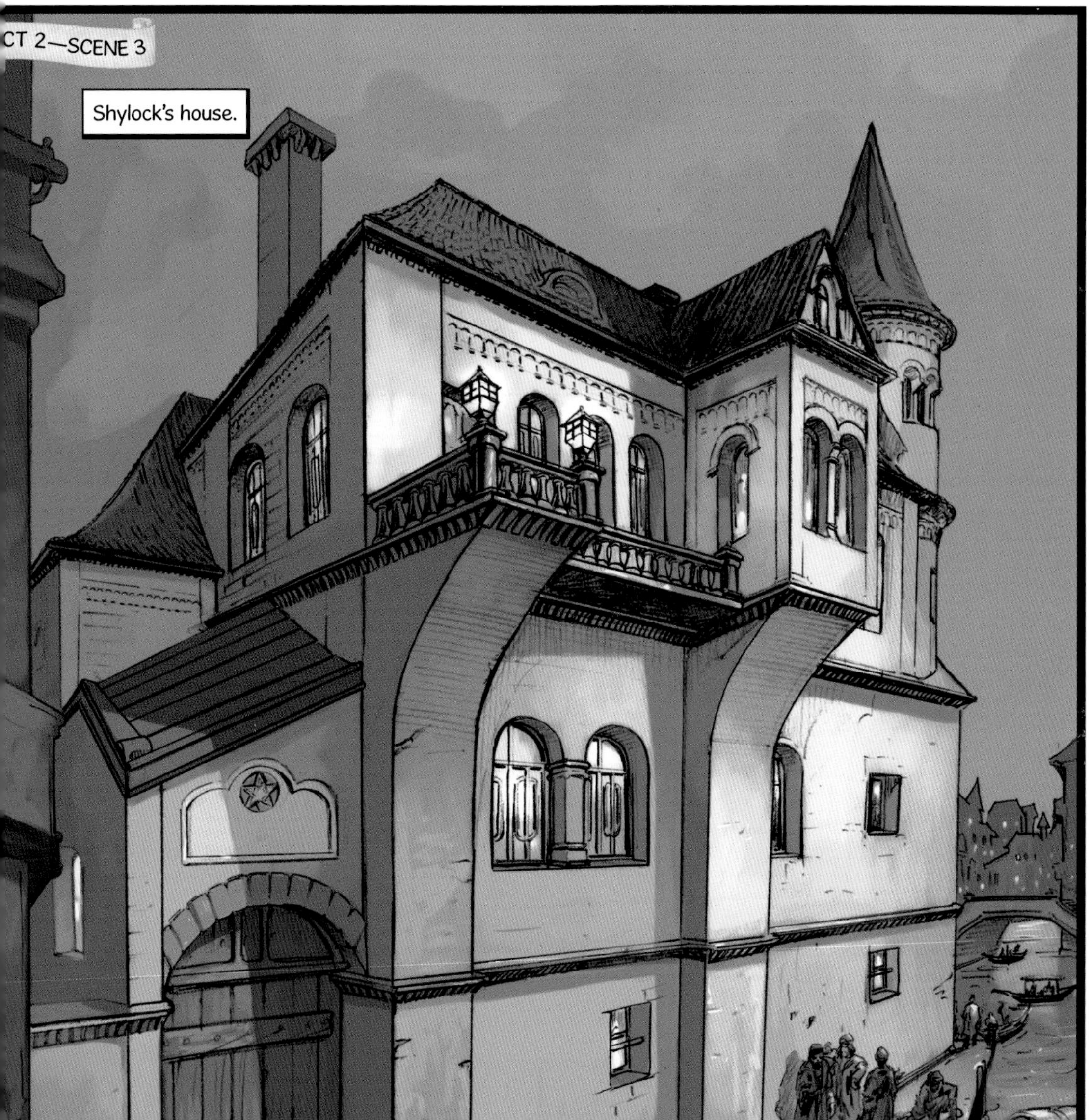

CT 2—SCENE 3
Shylock's house.

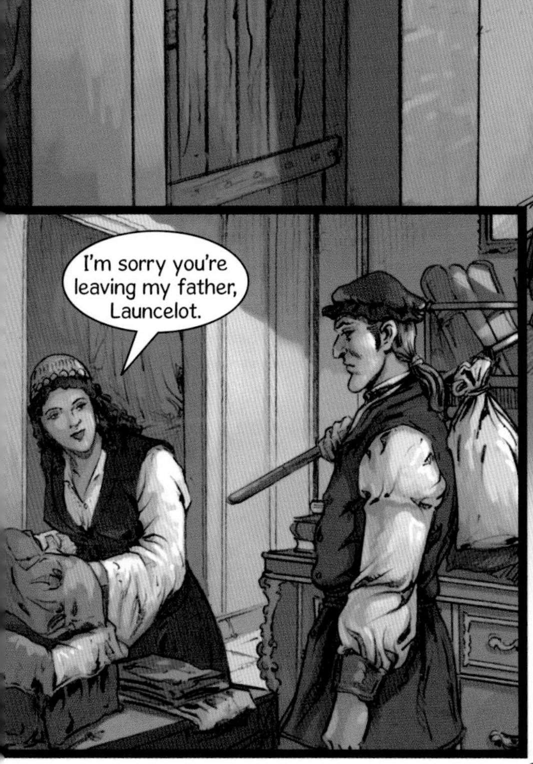

I'm sorry you're leaving my father, Launcelot.

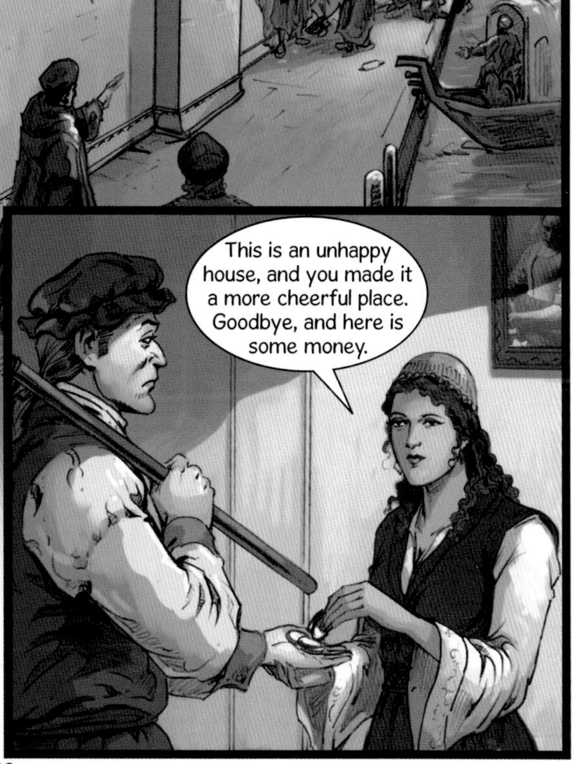

This is an unhappy house, and you made it a more cheerful place. Goodbye, and here is some money.

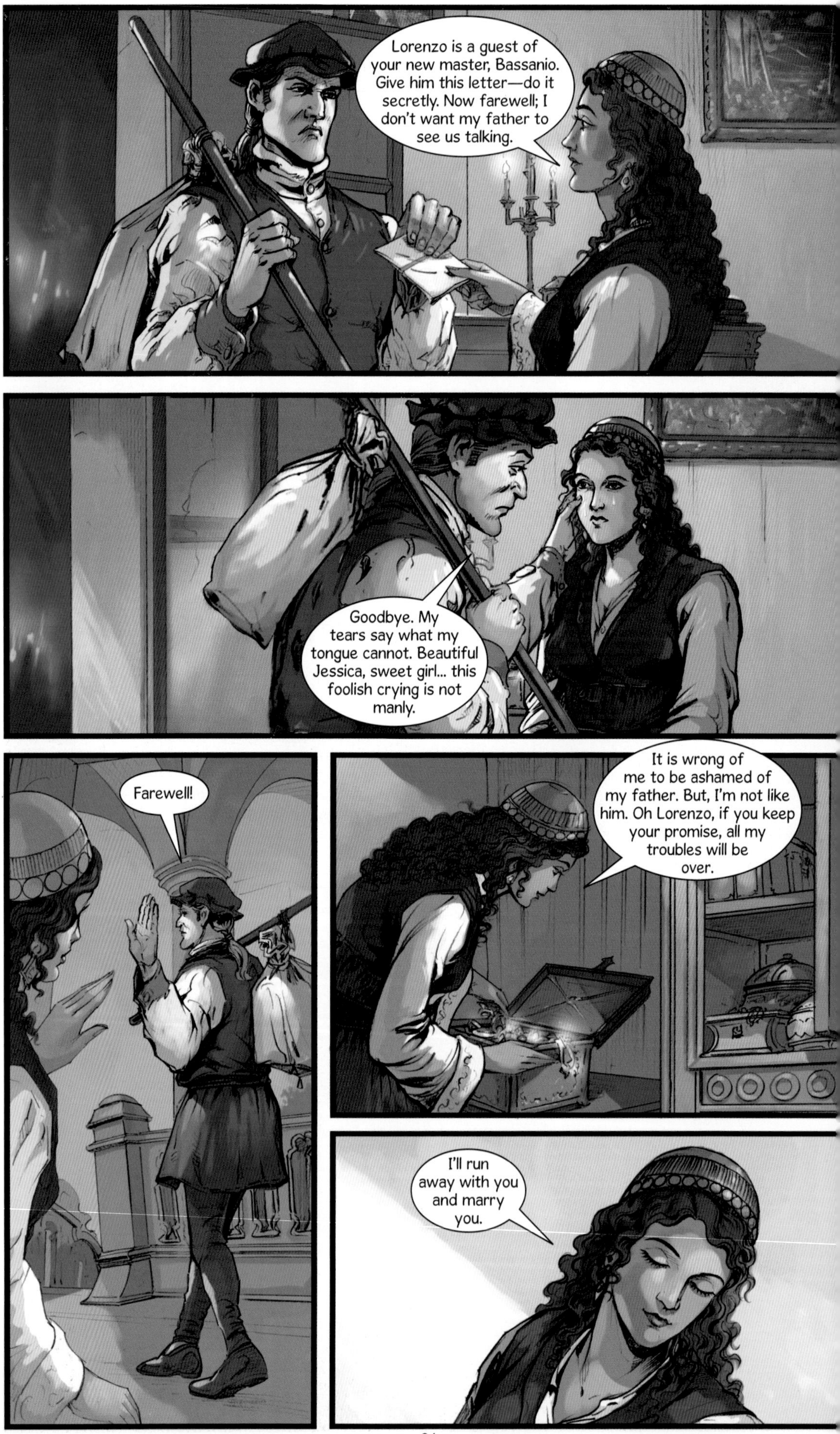
Lorenzo is a guest of your new master, Bassanio. Give him this letter—do it secretly. Now farewell; I don't want my father to see us talking.
Goodbye. My tears say what my tongue cannot. Beautiful Jessica, sweet girl... this foolish crying is not manly.
Farewell!
It is wrong of me to be ashamed of my father. But, I'm not like him. Oh Lorenzo, if you keep your promise, all my troubles will be over.
I'll run away with you and marry you.

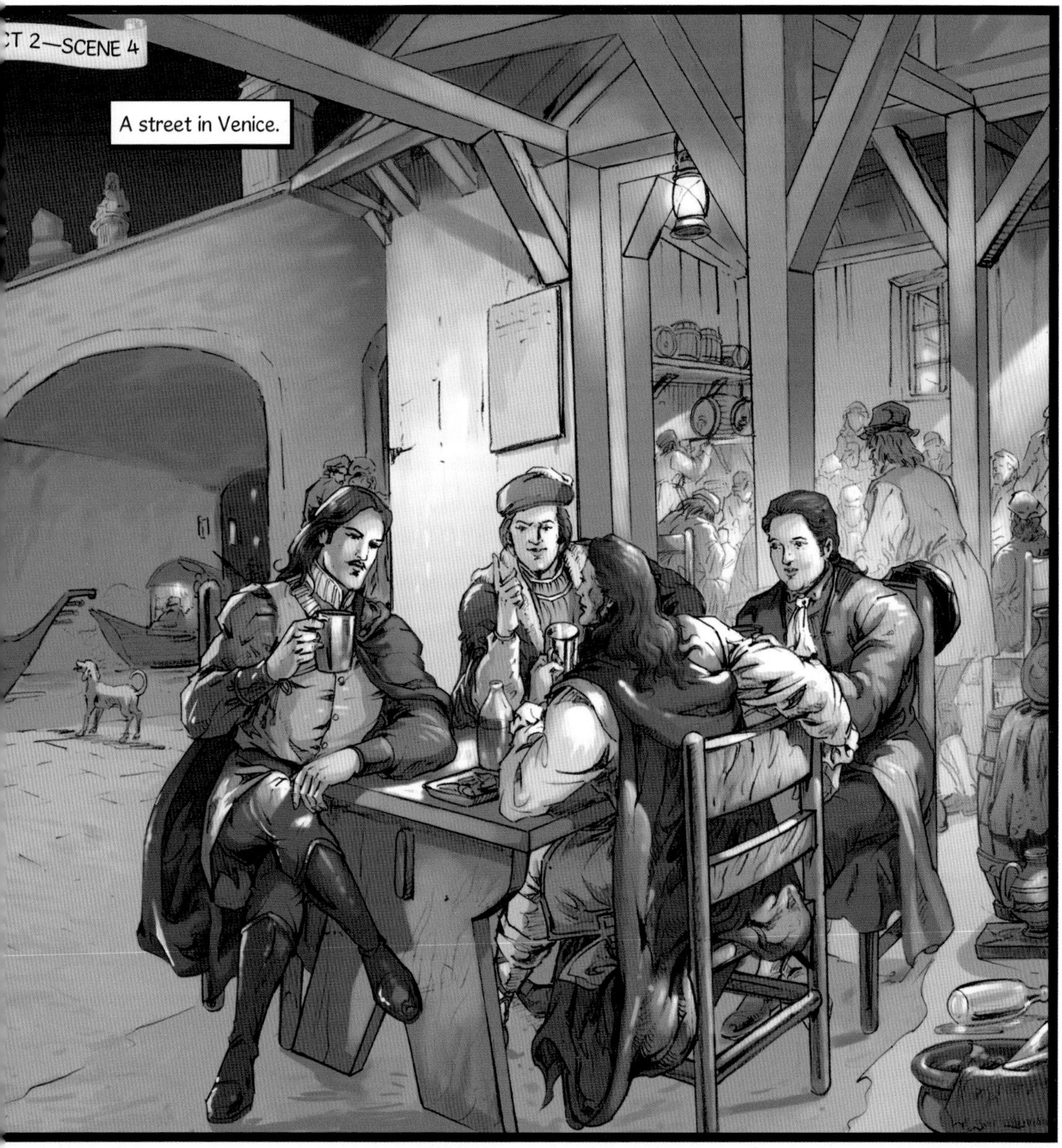
CT 2—SCENE 4
A street in Venice.

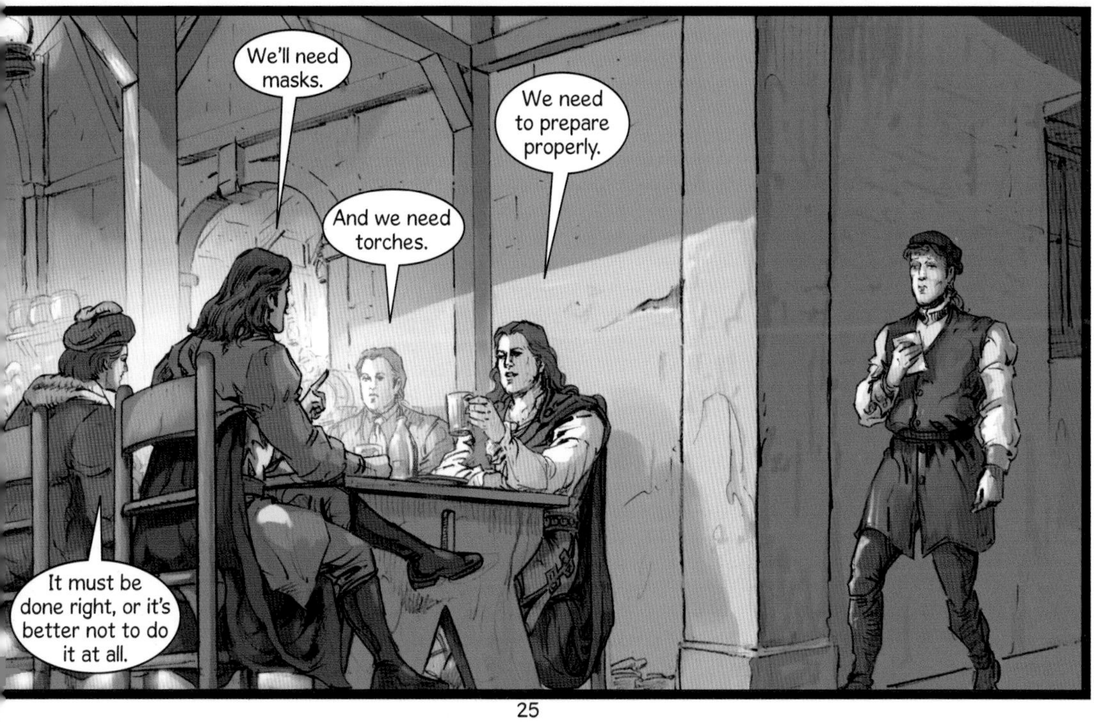
We'll need masks.
And we need torches.
We need to prepare properly.
It must be done right, or it's better not to do it at all.

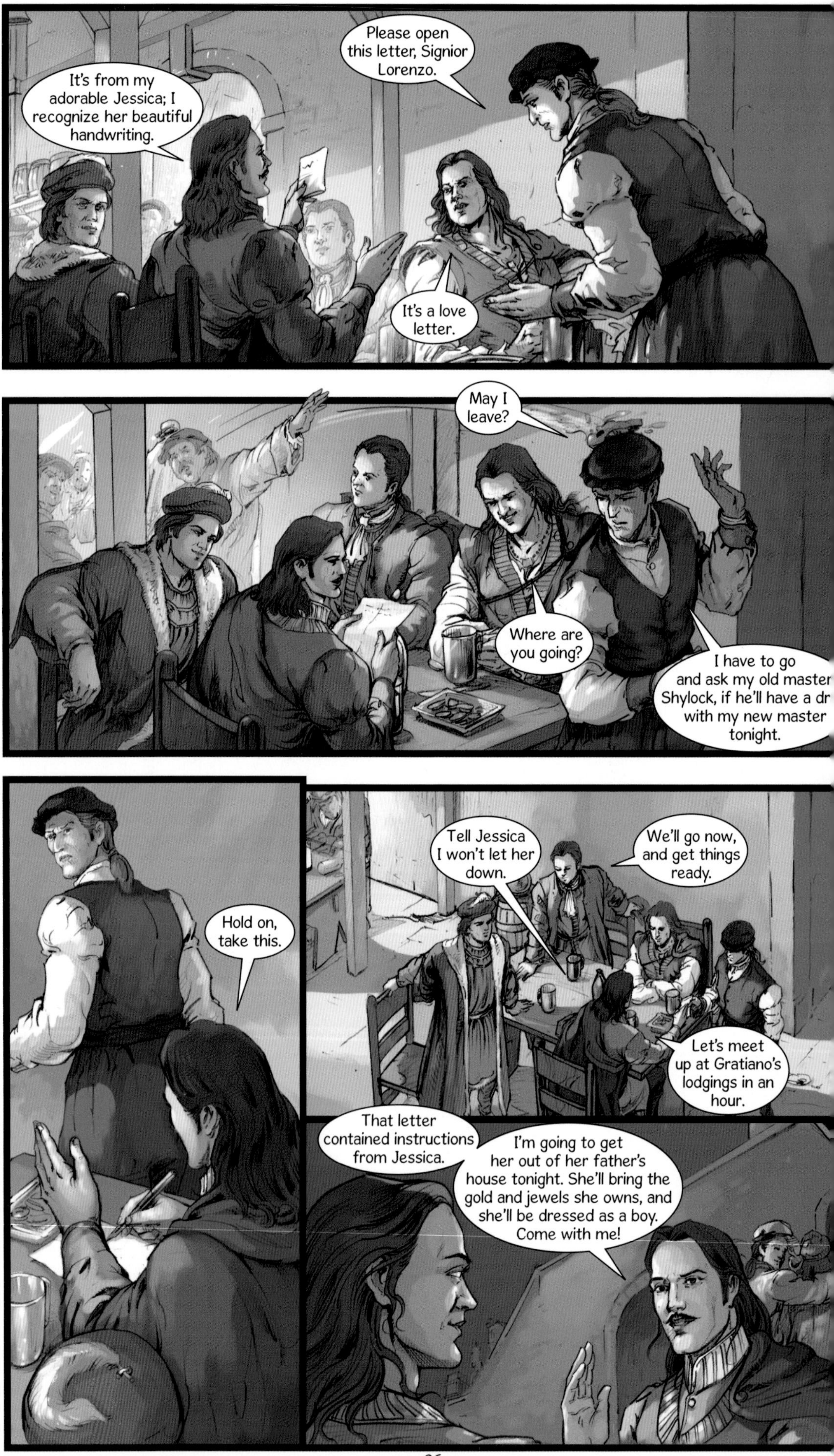
Please open this letter, Signior Lorenzo.
It's from my adorable Jessica; I recognize her beautiful handwriting.
It's a love letter.
May I leave?
Where are you going?
I have to go and ask my old master Shylock, if he'll have a dr with my new master tonight.
Hold on, take this.
Tell Jessica I won't let her down.
We'll go now, and get things ready.
Let's meet up at Gratiano's lodgings in an hour.
That letter contained instructions from Jessica.
I'm going to get her out of her father's house tonight. She'll bring the gold and jewels she owns, and she'll be dressed as a boy. Come with me!

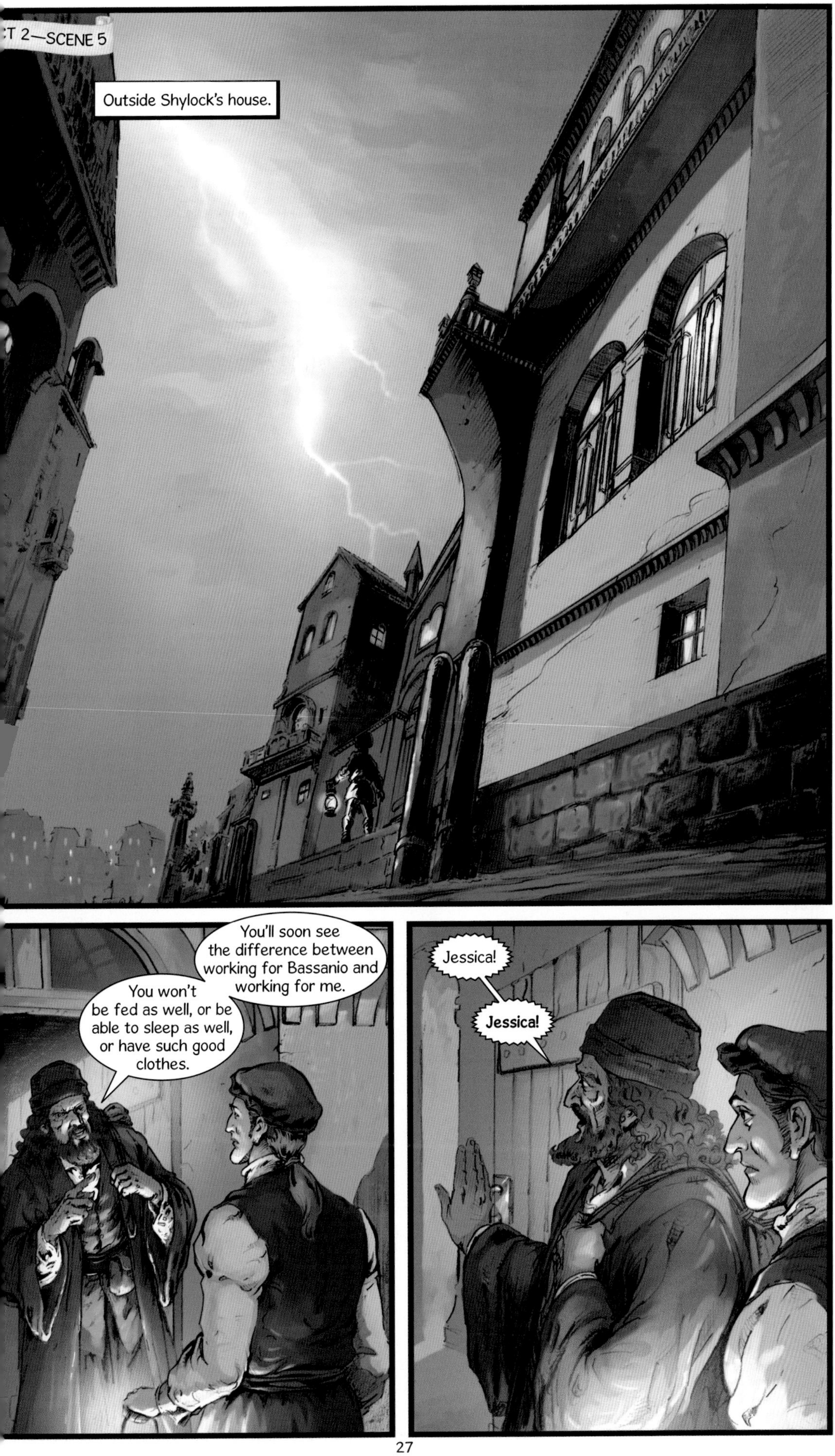

T 2—SCENE 5
Outside Shylock's house.
You'll soon see the difference between working for Bassanio and working for me.
You won't be fed as well, or be able to sleep as well, or have such good clothes.
Jessica!
Jessica!

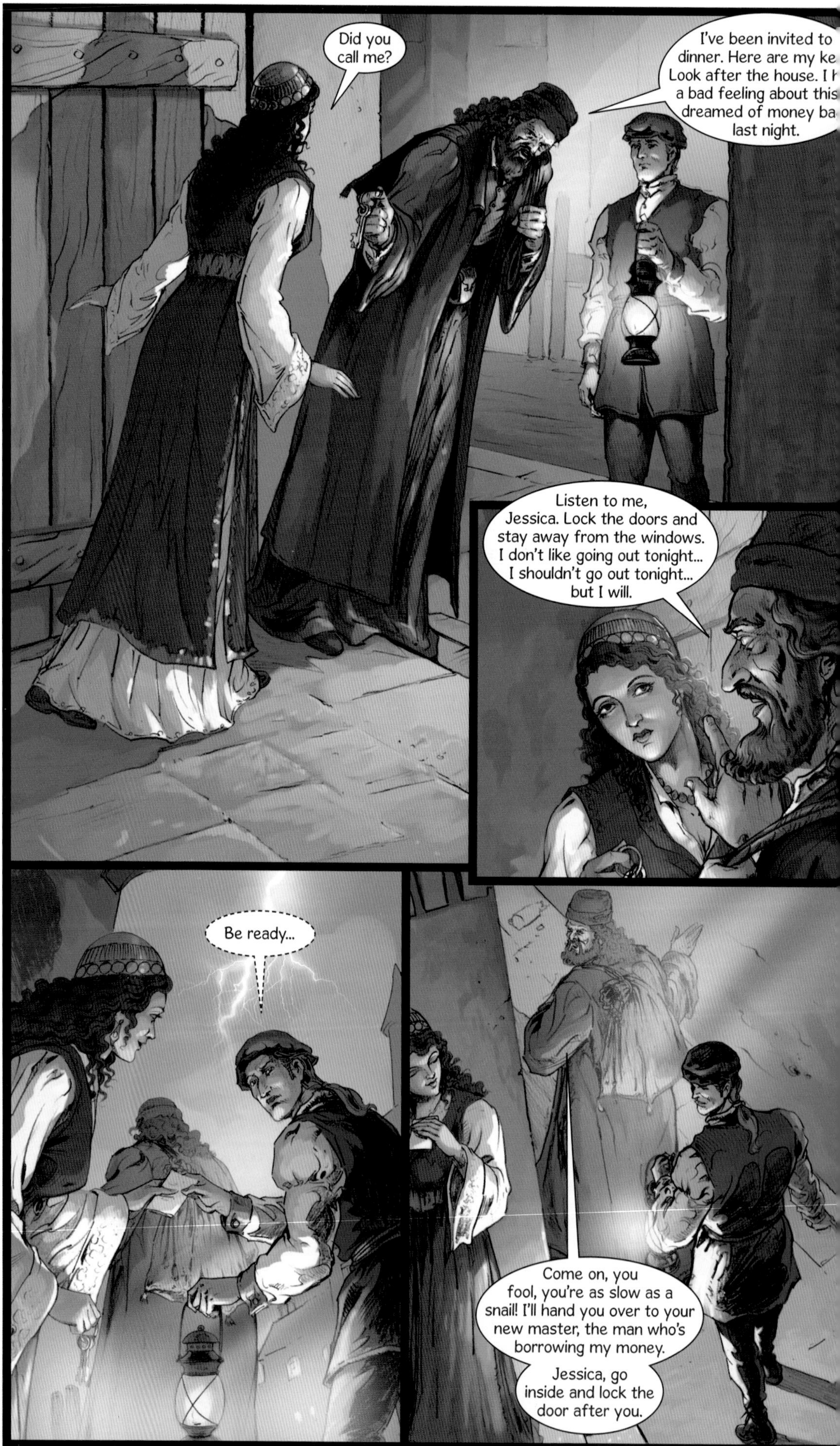
Did you call me?
I've been invited to dinner. Here are my ke Look after the house. I h a bad feeling about this dreamed of money ba last night.
Listen to me, Jessica. Lock the doors and stay away from the windows. I don't like going out tonight... I shouldn't go out tonight... but I will.
Be ready...
Come on, you fool, you're as slow as a snail! I'll hand you over to your new master, the man who's borrowing my money.
Jessica, go inside and lock the door after you.

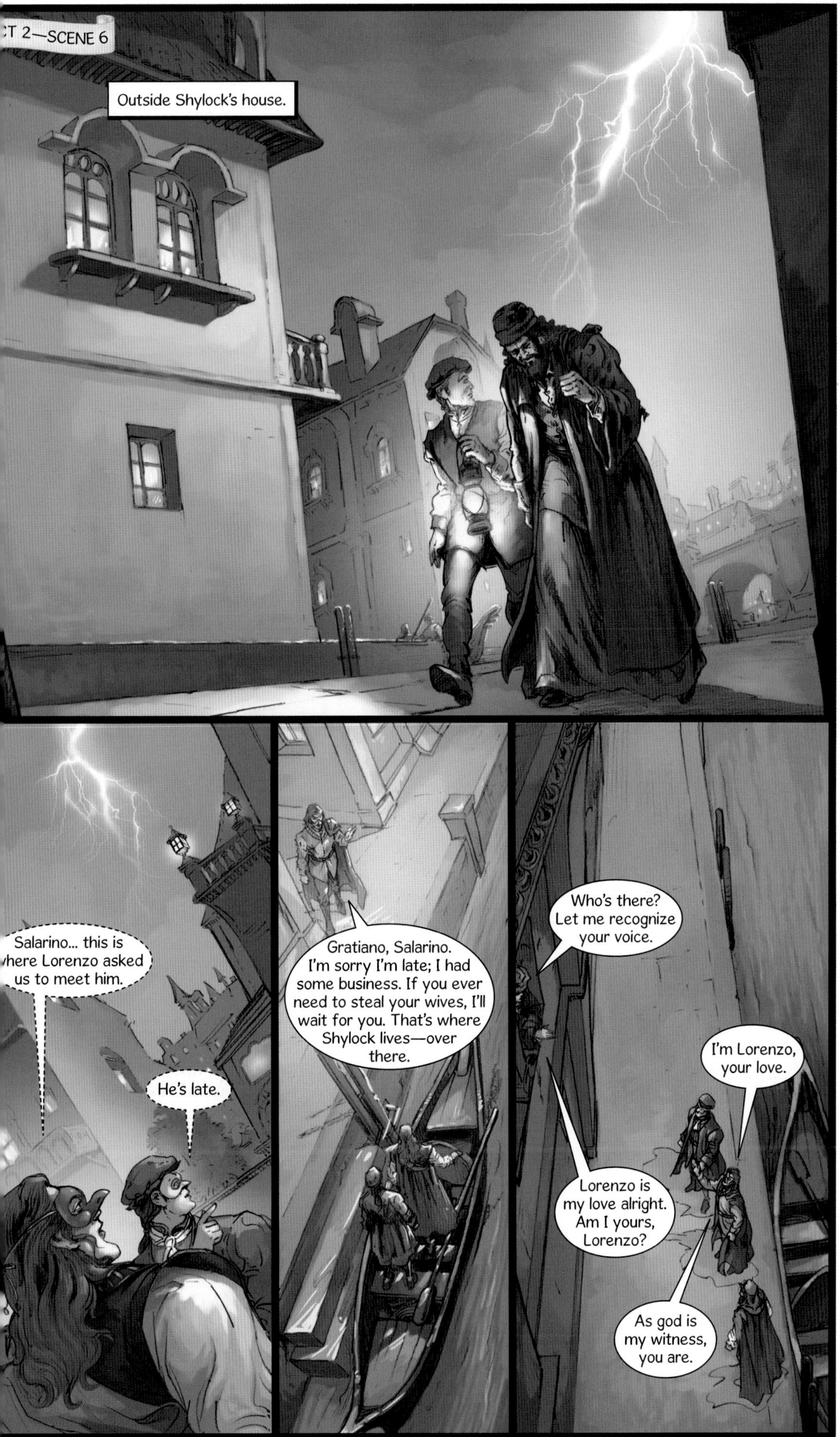

T 2—SCENE 6
Outside Shylock's house.
Salarino... this is here Lorenzo asked us to meet him.
He's late.
Gratiano, Salarino. I'm sorry I'm late; I had some business. If you ever need to steal your wives, I'll wait for you. That's where Shylock lives—over there.
Who's there? Let me recognize your voice.
I'm Lorenzo, your love.
Lorenzo is my love alright. Am I yours, Lorenzo?
As god is my witness, you are.

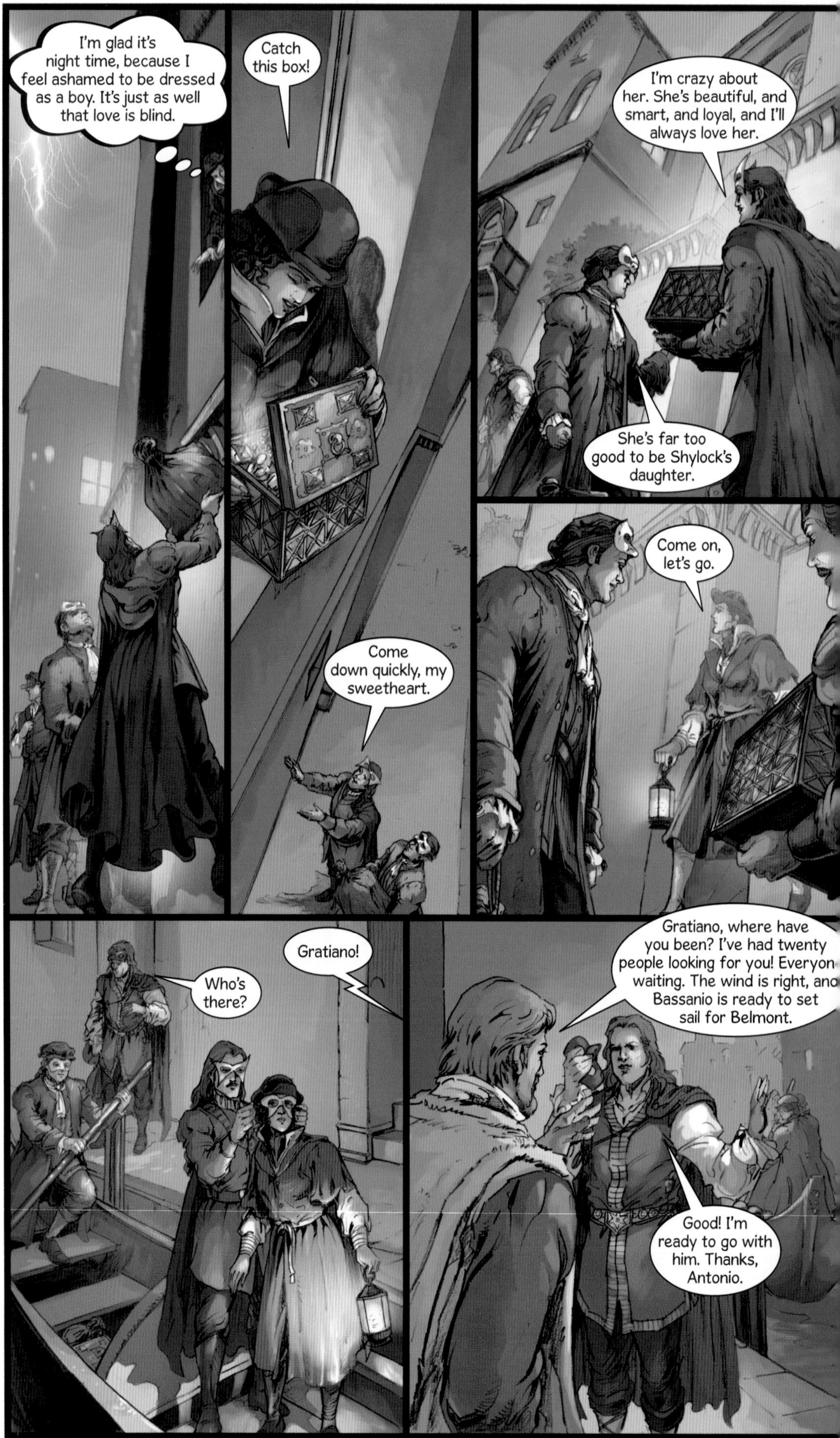

I'm glad it's night time, because I feel ashamed to be dressed as a boy. It's just as well that love is blind.
Catch this box!
Come down quickly, my sweetheart.
I'm crazy about her. She's beautiful, and smart, and loyal, and I'll always love her.
She's far too good to be Shylock's daughter.
Come on, let's go.
Who's there?
Gratiano!
Gratiano, where have you been? I've had twenty people looking for you! Everyon waiting. The wind is right, and Bassanio is ready to set sail for Belmont.
Good! I'm ready to go with him. Thanks, Antonio.

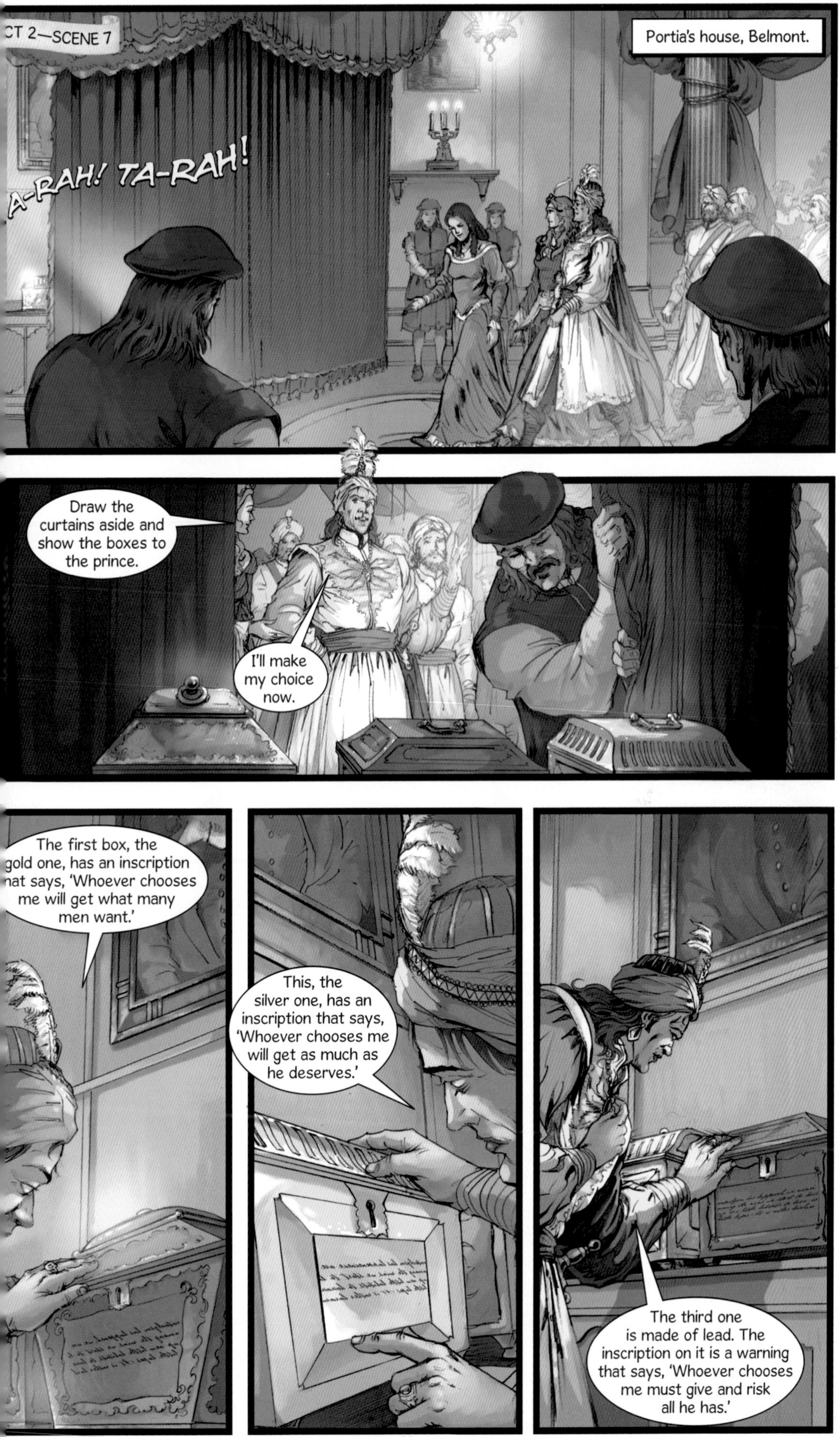
CT 2—SCENE 7
Portia's house, Belmont.
A-RAH! TA-RAH!
Draw the curtains aside and show the boxes to the prince.
I'll make my choice now.
The first box, the gold one, has an inscription that says, 'Whoever chooses me will get what many men want.'
This, the silver one, has an inscription that says, 'Whoever chooses me will get as much as he deserves.'
The third one is made of lead. The inscription on it is a warning that says, 'Whoever chooses me must give and risk all he has.'

One of them has my picture inside. If you choose that one, you may marry me.

God, help me choose! I must read the inscriptions again!

'Whoever chooses me must give and risk all he has.' For lead? This box is too threatening. A prince like m wouldn't choose something so worthless. I won't risk everything for lead.

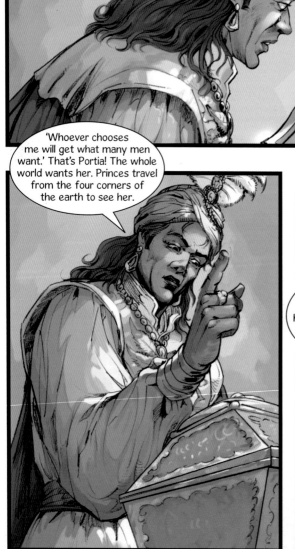

'Whoever chooses me will get as much he deserves.' I deserve Portia. What if I choose this one? Before I decide, I'll read the gold one again.

'Whoever chooses me will get what many men want.' That's Portia! The whole world wants her. Princes travel from the four corners of the earth to see her.

Her picture is inside one of these boxes. The lead one? No, lead's too common to hold her. Is she in the silver one? No, silver is far less valuable than gold. She must be in the gold one!

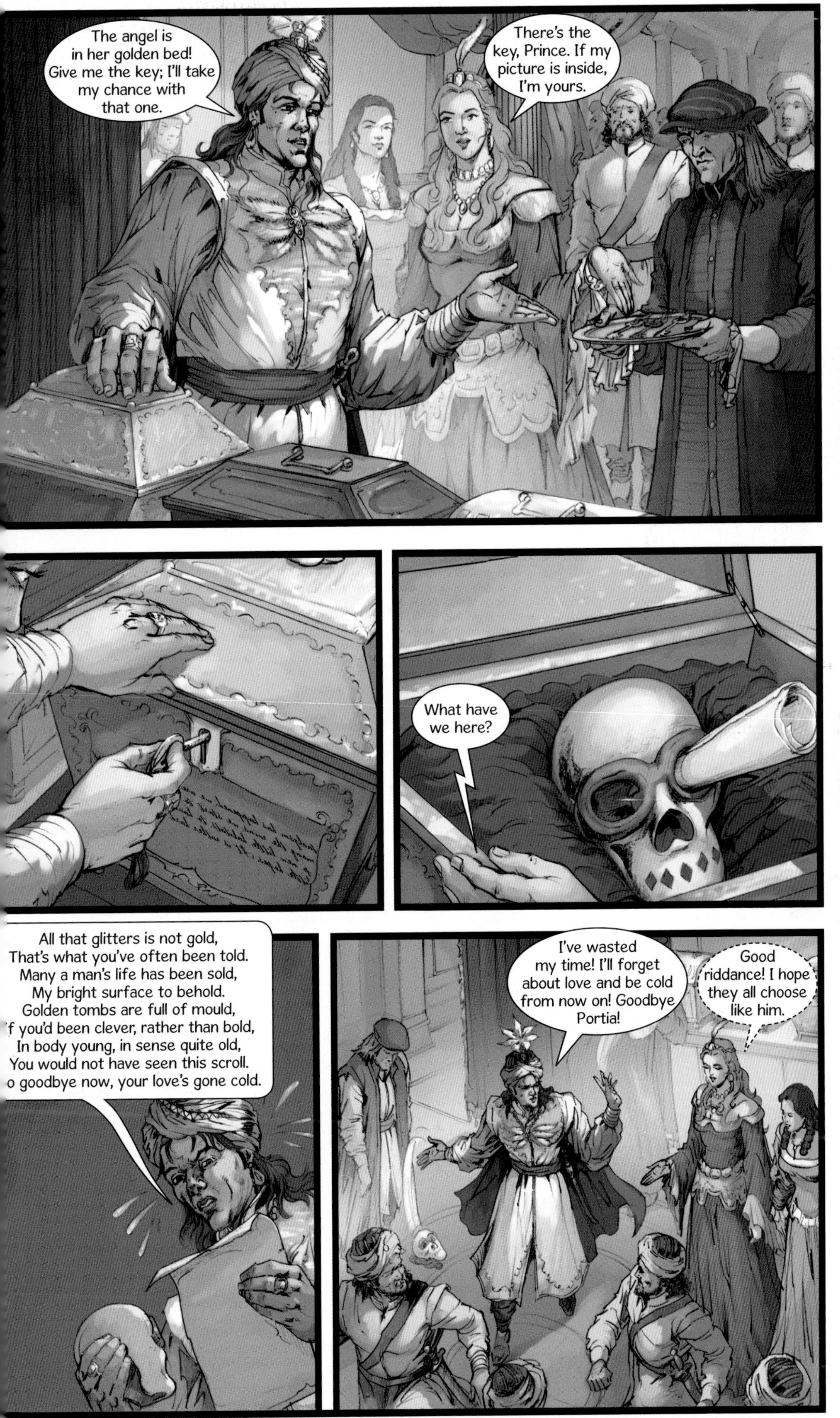
The angel is in her golden bed! Give me the key; I'll take my chance with that one.
There's the key, Prince. If my picture is inside, I'm yours.
What have we here?
All that glitters is not gold,
That's what you've often been told.
Many a man's life has been sold,
My bright surface to behold.
Golden tombs are full of mould,
f you'd been clever, rather than bold,
In body young, in sense quite old,
You would not have seen this scroll.
o goodbye now, your love's gone cold.
I've wasted my time! I'll forget about love and be cold from now on! Goodbye Portia!
Good riddance! I hope they all choose like him.

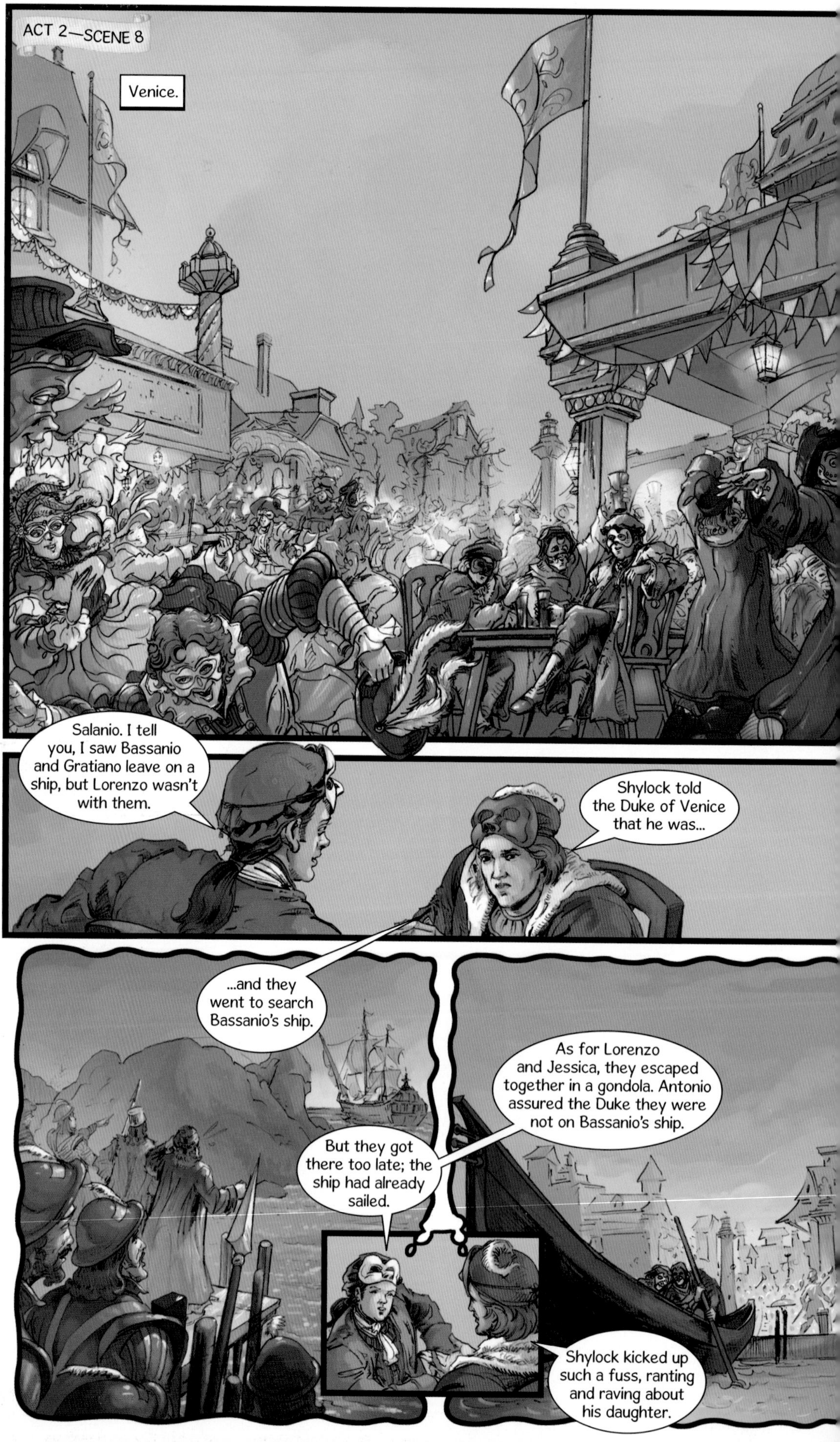

ACT 2—SCENE 8
Venice.
Salanio. I tell you, I saw Bassanio and Gratiano leave on a ship, but Lorenzo wasn't with them.
Shylock told the Duke of Venice that he was...
...and they went to search Bassanio's ship.
But they got there too late; the ship had already sailed.
As for Lorenzo and Jessica, they escaped together in a gondola. Antonio assured the Duke they were not on Bassanio's ship.
Shylock kicked up such a fuss, ranting and raving about his daughter.

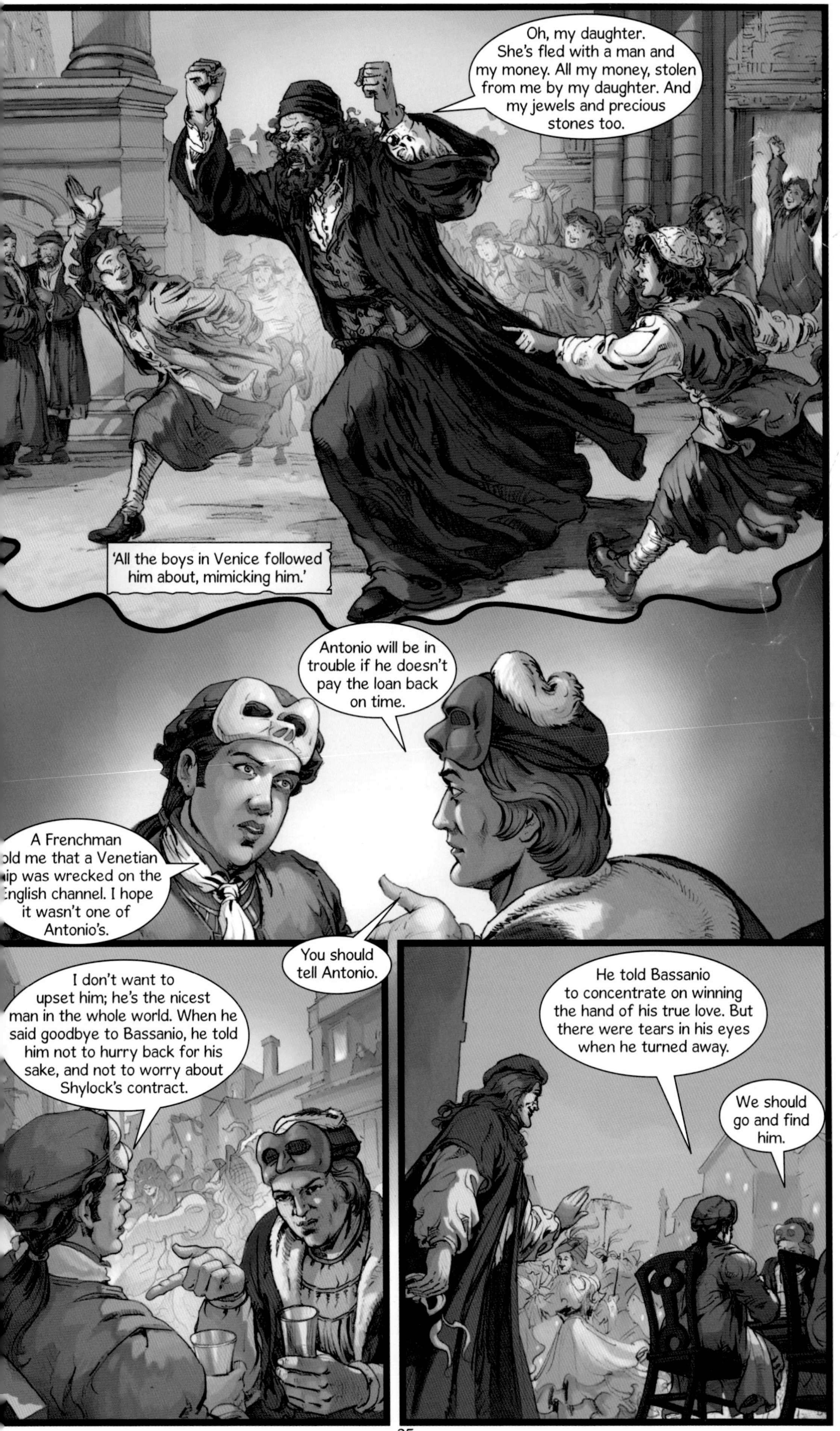
Oh, my daughter. She's fled with a man and my money. All my money, stolen from me by my daughter. And my jewels and precious stones too.
'All the boys in Venice followed him about, mimicking him.'
Antonio will be in trouble if he doesn't pay the loan back on time.
A Frenchman old me that a Venetian ip was wrecked on the nglish channel. I hope it wasn't one of Antonio's.
You should tell Antonio.
I don't want to upset him; he's the nicest man in the whole world. When he said goodbye to Bassanio, he told him not to hurry back for his sake, and not to worry about Shylock's contract.
He told Bassanio to concentrate on winning the hand of his true love. But there were tears in his eyes when he turned away.
We should go and find him.

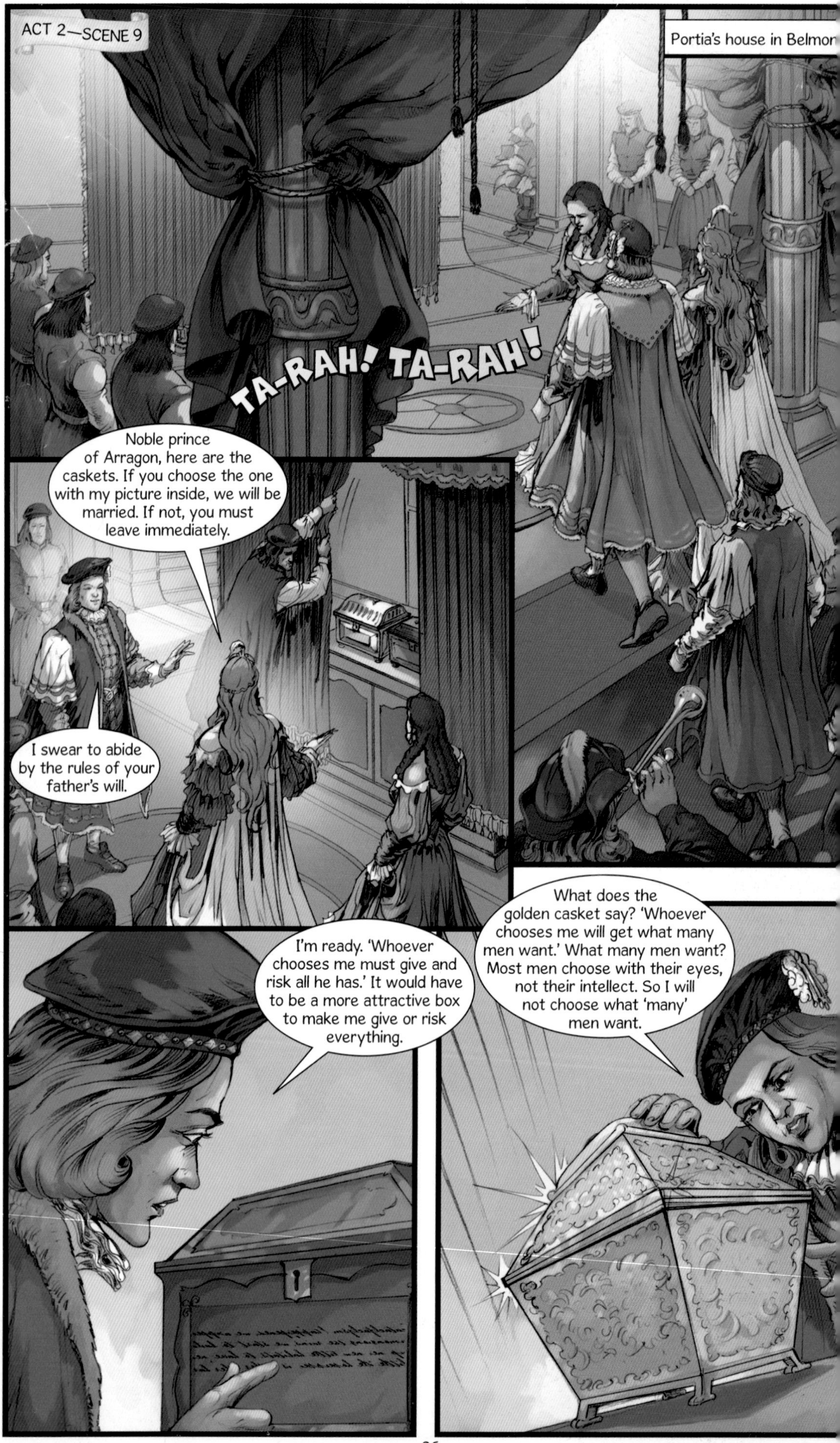
ACT 2—SCENE 9
Portia's house in Belmon
TA-RAH! TA-RAH!
Noble prince of Arragon, here are the caskets. If you choose the one with my picture inside, we will be married. If not, you must leave immediately.
I swear to abide by the rules of your father's will.
I'm ready. 'Whoever chooses me must give and risk all he has.' It would have to be a more attractive box to make me give or risk everything.
What does the golden casket say? 'Whoever chooses me will get what many men want.' What many men want? Most men choose with their eyes, not their intellect. So I will not choose what 'many' men want.

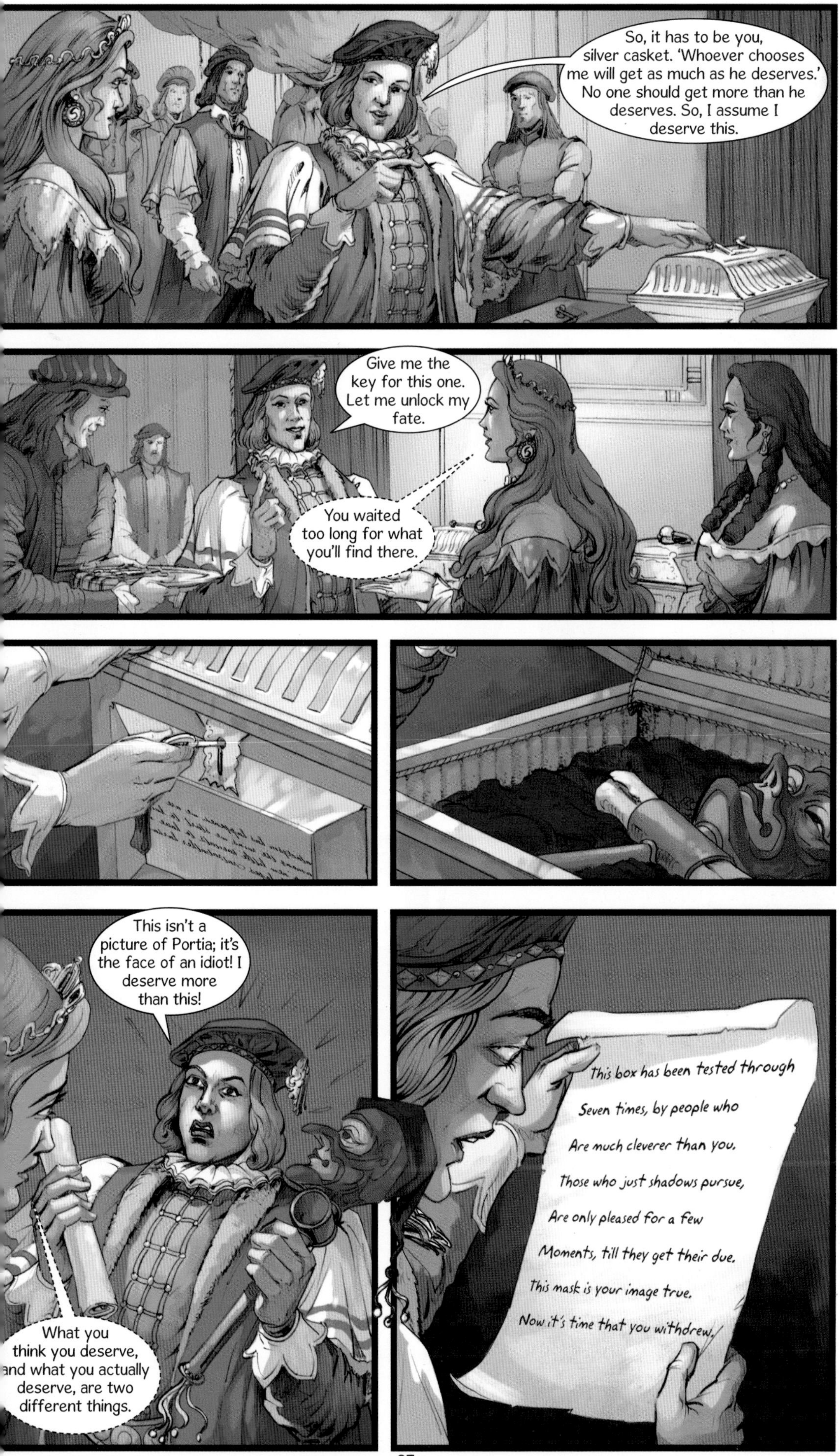

So, it has to be you, silver casket. 'Whoever chooses me will get as much as he deserves.' No one should get more than he deserves. So, I assume I deserve this.
Give me the key for this one. Let me unlock my fate.
You waited too long for what you'll find there.
This isn't a picture of Portia; it's the face of an idiot! I deserve more than this!
What you think you deserve, and what you actually deserve, are two different things.
This box has been tested through
Seven times, by people who
Are much cleverer than you.
Those who just shadows pursue,
Are only pleased for a few
Moments, till they get their due.
This mask is your image true.
Now it's time that you withdrew.

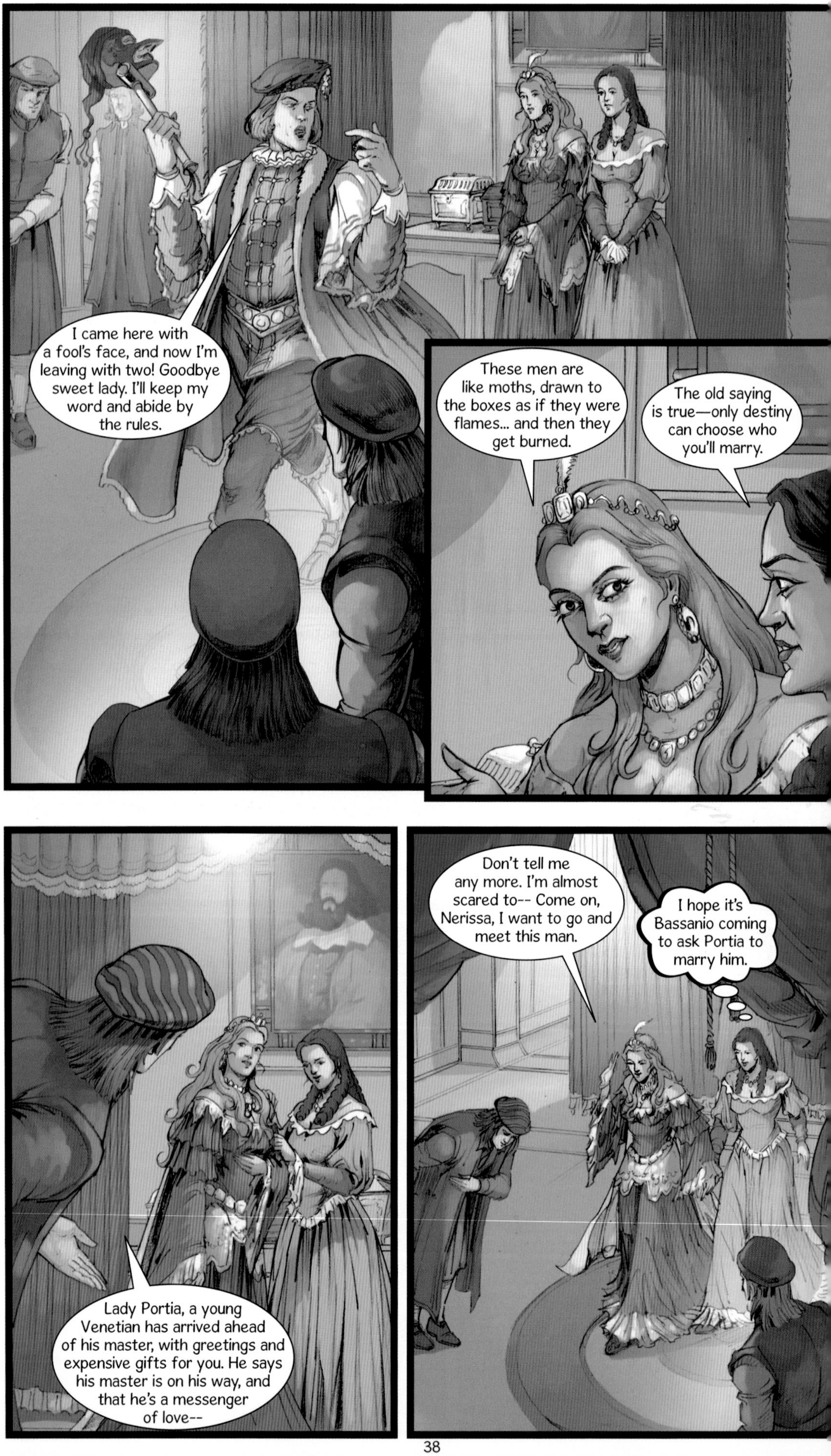
I came here with a fool's face, and now I'm leaving with two! Goodbye sweet lady. I'll keep my word and abide by the rules.
These men are like moths, drawn to the boxes as if they were flames... and then they get burned.
The old saying is true—only destiny can choose who you'll marry.
Lady Portia, a young Venetian has arrived ahead of his master, with greetings and expensive gifts for you. He says his master is on his way, and that he's a messenger of love--
Don't tell me any more. I'm almost scared to-- Come on, Nerissa, I want to go and meet this man.
I hope it's Bassanio coming to ask Portia to marry him.

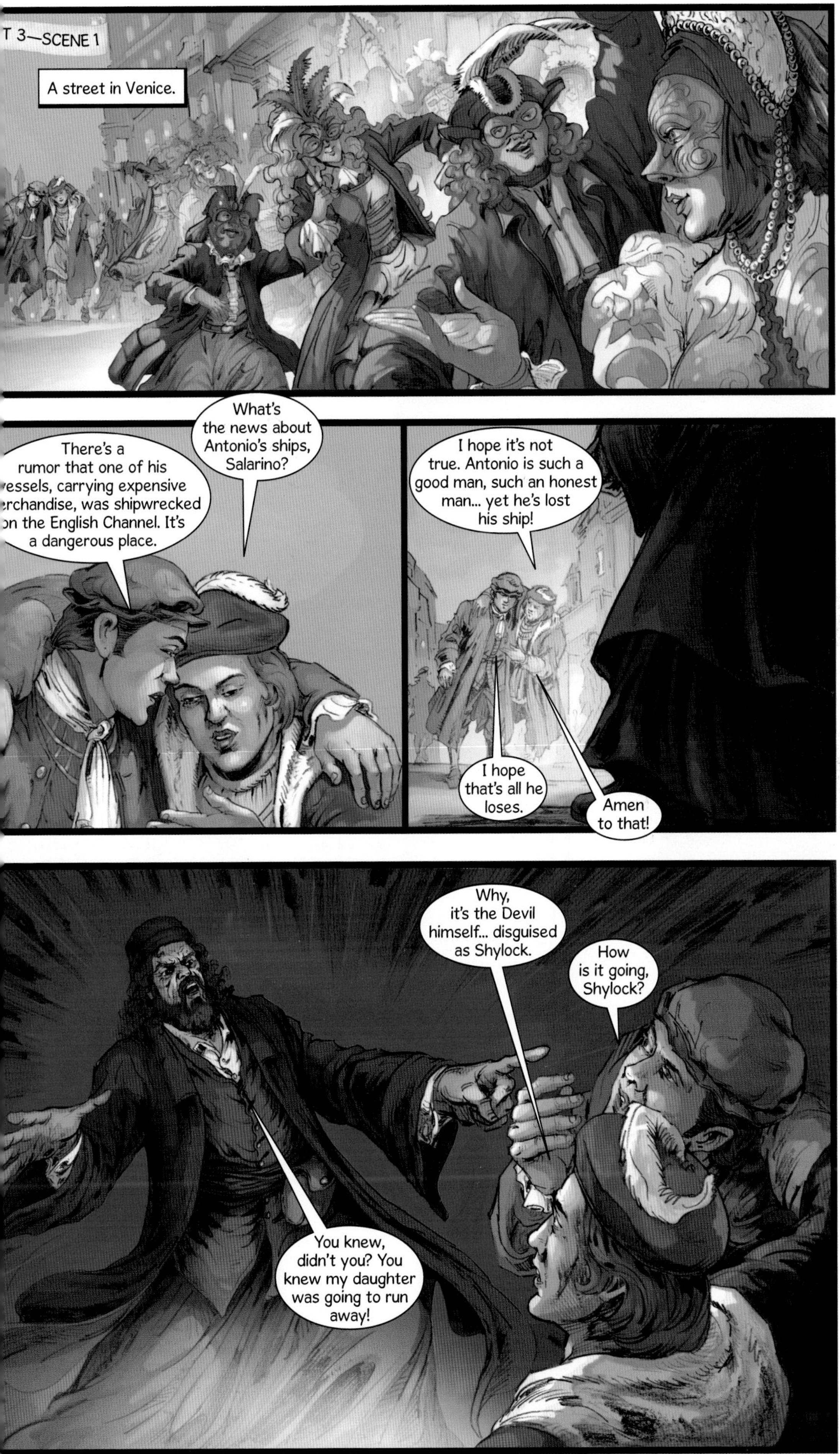
T 3—SCENE 1
A street in Venice.
What's the news about Antonio's ships, Salarino?
There's a rumor that one of his vessels, carrying expensive erchandise, was shipwrecked on the English Channel. It's a dangerous place.
I hope it's not true. Antonio is such a good man, such an honest man... yet he's lost his ship!
I hope that's all he loses.
Amen to that!
Why, it's the Devil himself... disguised as Shylock.
How is it going, Shylock?
You knew, didn't you? You knew my daughter was going to run away!

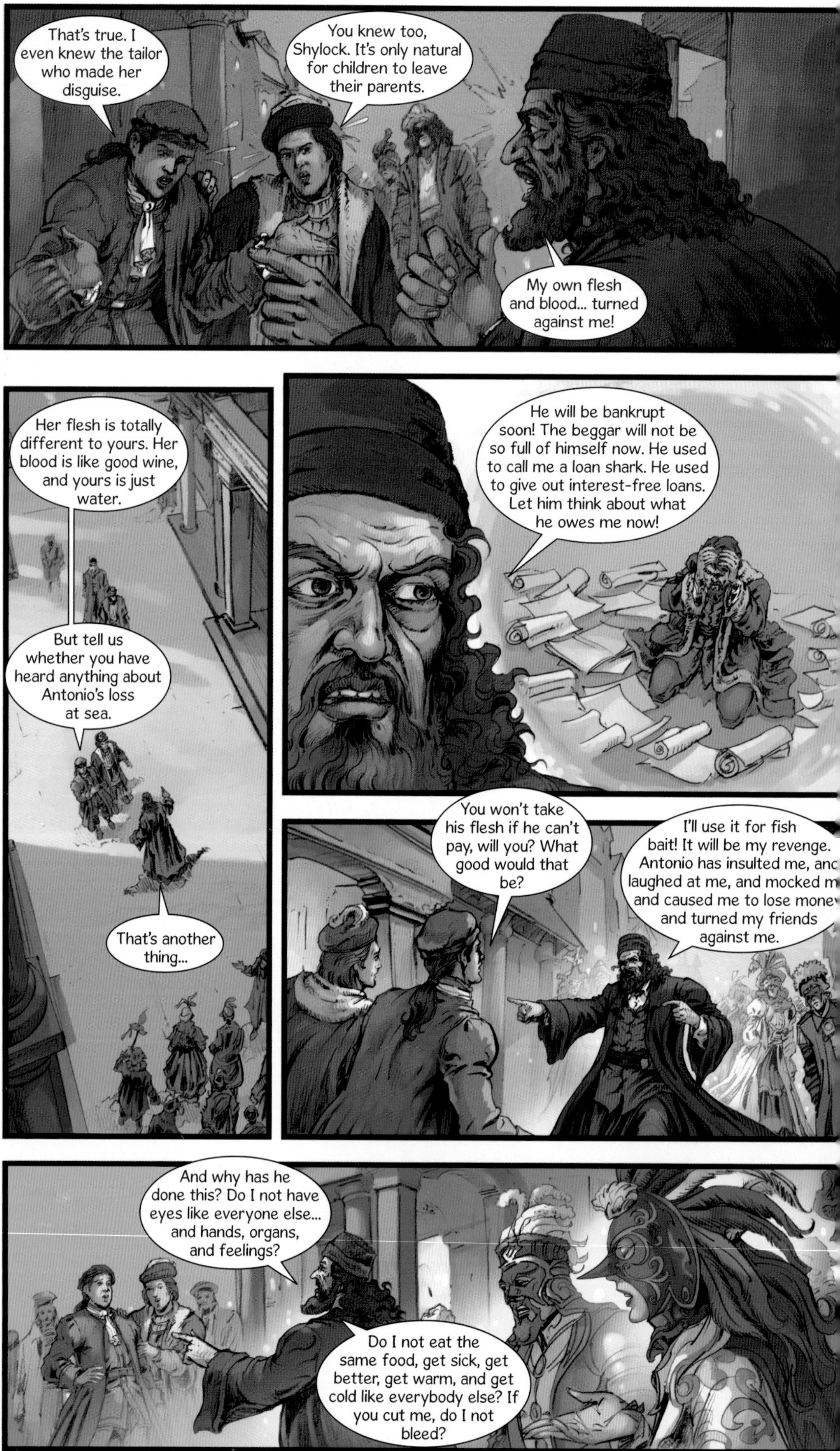
That's true. I even knew the tailor who made her disguise.
You knew too, Shylock. It's only natural for children to leave their parents.
My own flesh and blood... turned against me!
Her flesh is totally different to yours. Her blood is like good wine, and yours is just water.
But tell us whether you have heard anything about Antonio's loss at sea.
That's another thing...
He will be bankrupt soon! The beggar will not be so full of himself now. He used to call me a loan shark. He used to give out interest-free loans. Let him think about what he owes me now!
You won't take his flesh if he can't pay, will you? What good would that be?
I'll use it for fish bait! It will be my revenge. Antonio has insulted me, anc laughed at me, and mocked m and caused me to lose mone and turned my friends against me.
And why has he done this? Do I not have eyes like everyone else... and hands, organs, and feelings?
Do I not eat the same food, get sick, get better, get warm, and get cold like everybody else? If you cut me, do I not bleed?

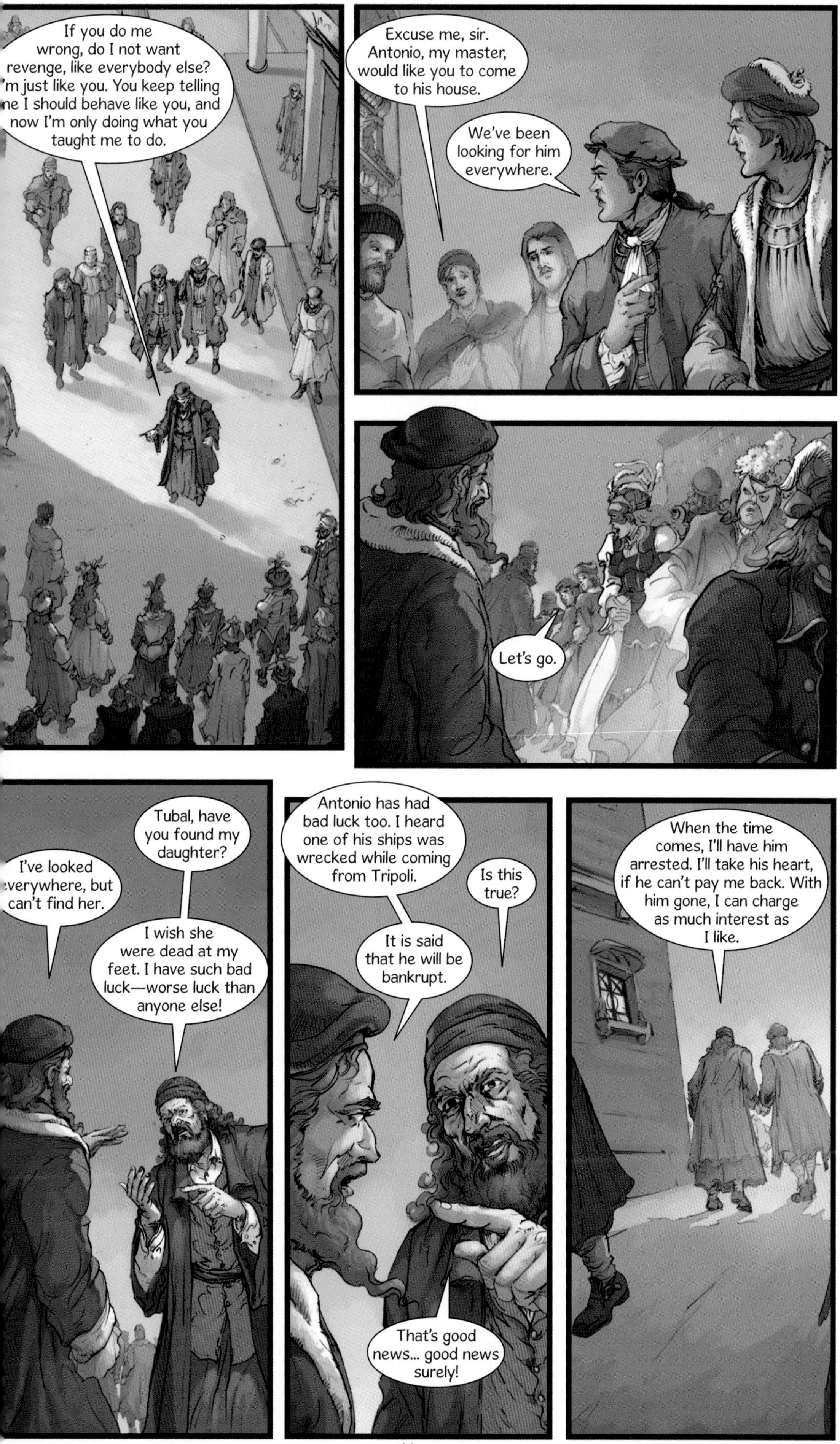

If you do me wrong, do I not want revenge, like everybody else? 'm just like you. You keep telling ne I should behave like you, and now I'm only doing what you taught me to do.
Excuse me, sir. Antonio, my master, would like you to come to his house.
We've been looking for him everywhere.
Let's go.
Tubal, have you found my daughter?
I've looked verywhere, but can't find her.
I wish she were dead at my feet. I have such bad luck—worse luck than anyone else!
Antonio has had bad luck too. I heard one of his ships was wrecked while coming from Tripoli.
Is this true?
It is said that he will be bankrupt.
That's good news... good news surely!
When the time comes, I'll have him arrested. I'll take his heart, if he can't pay me back. With him gone, I can charge as much interest as I like.

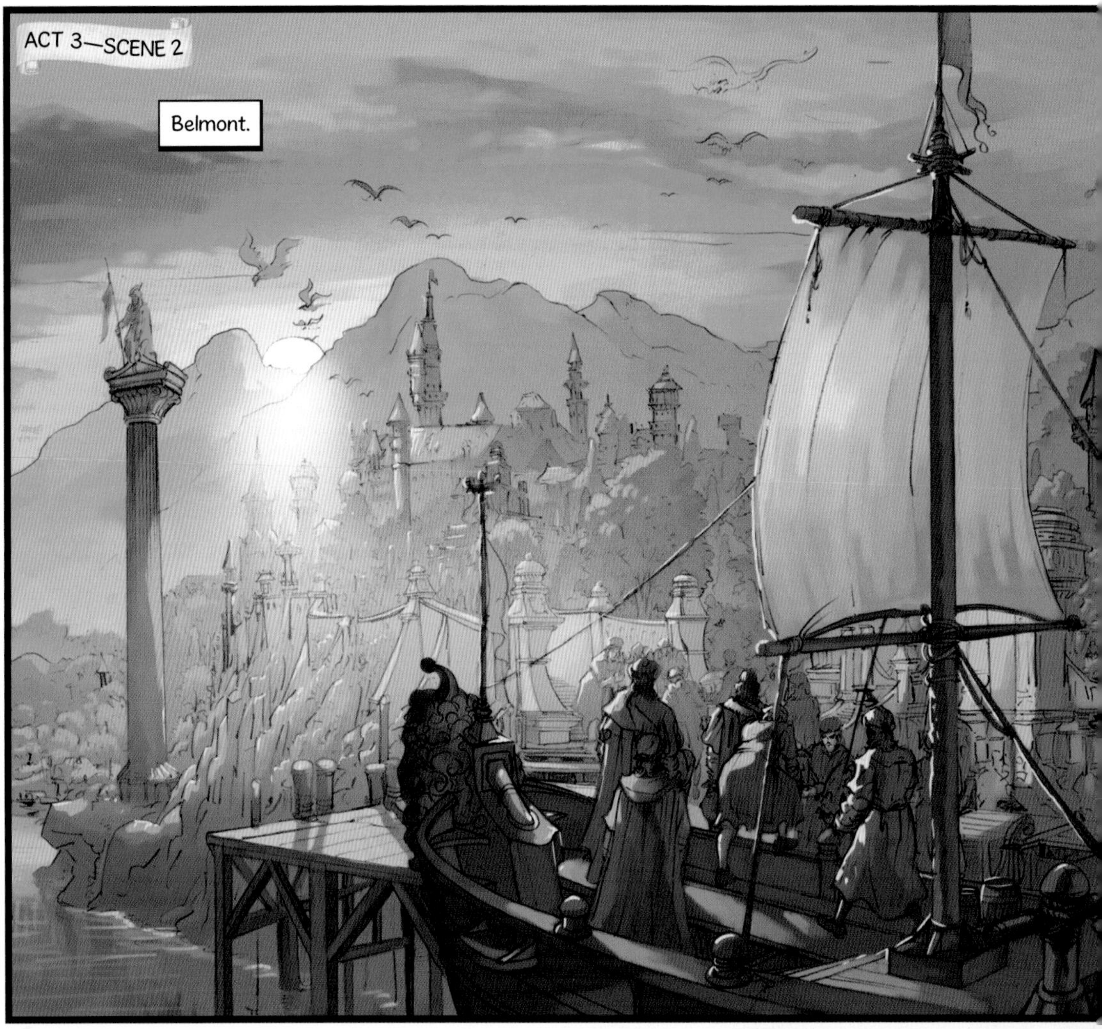
ACT 3—SCENE 2
Belmont.

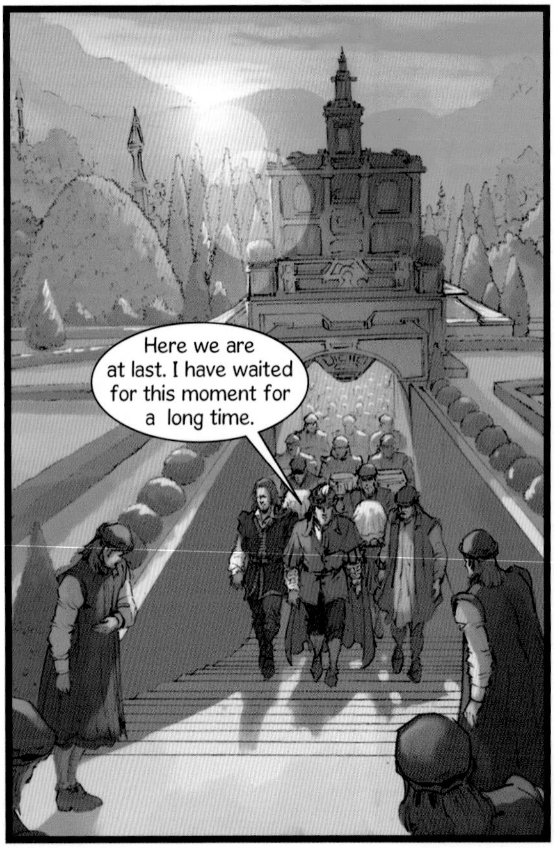
Here we are at last. I have waited for this moment for a long time.

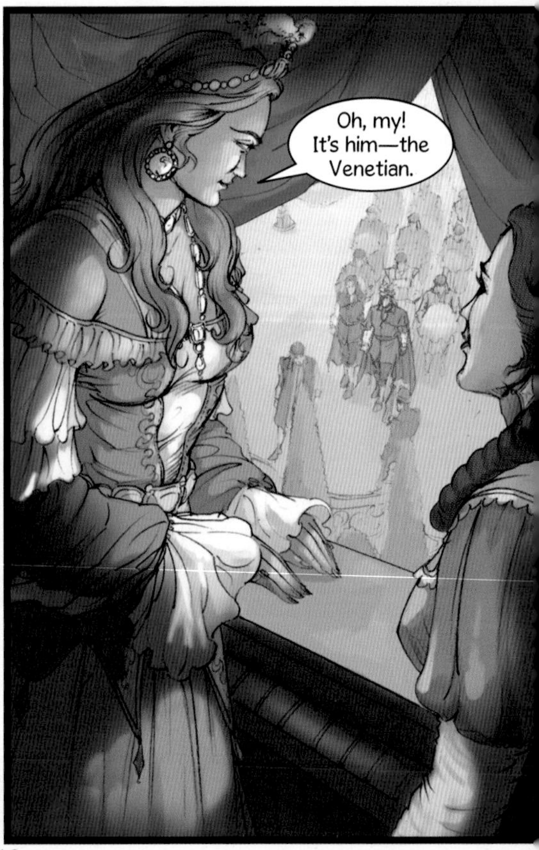
Oh, my! It's him—the Venetian.

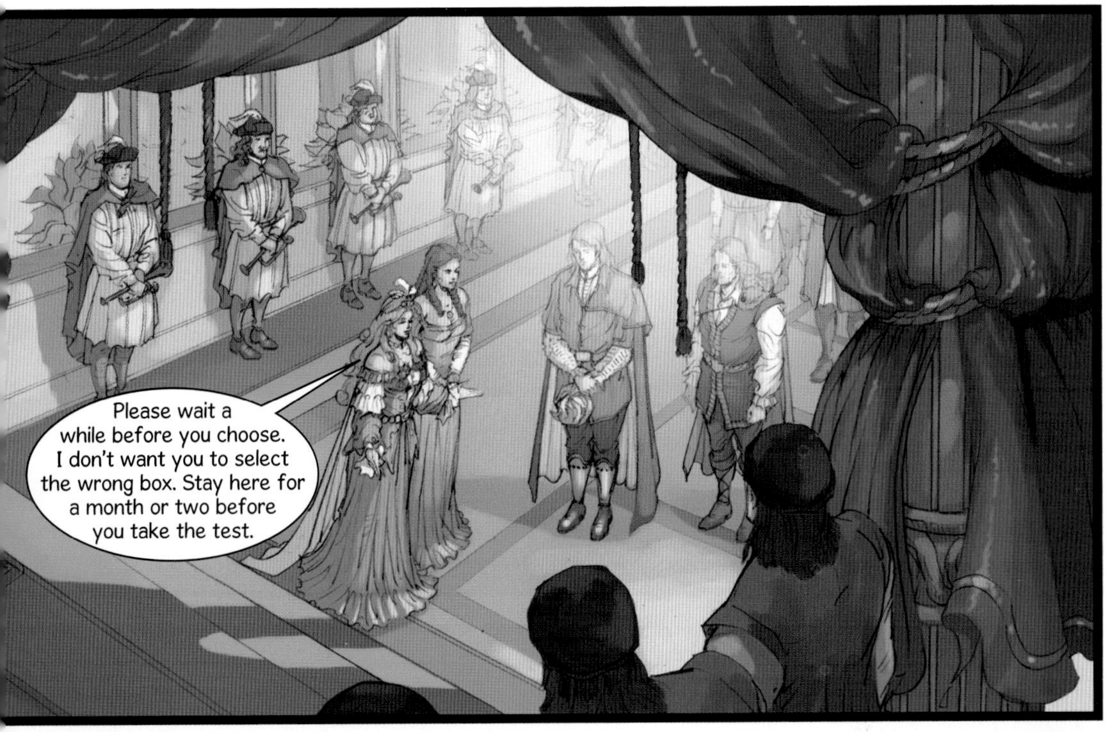
Please wait a while before you choose. I don't want you to select the wrong box. Stay here for a month or two before you take the test.

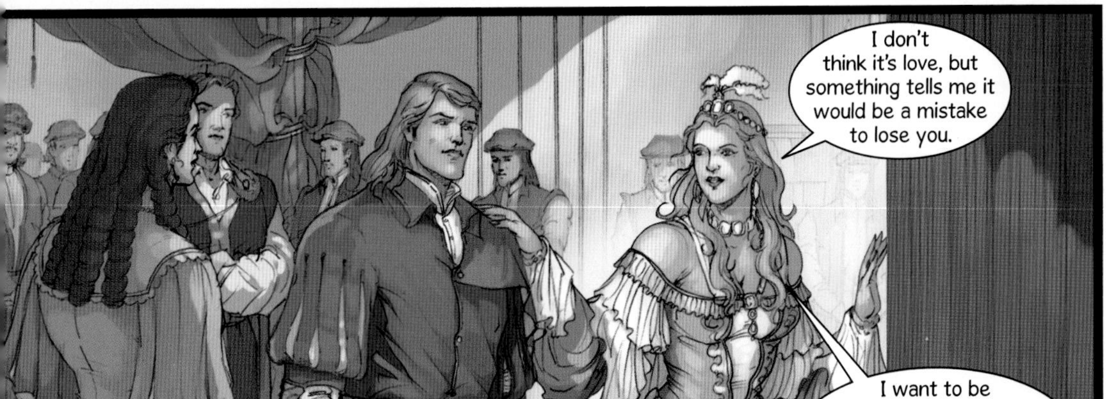
I don't think it's love, but something tells me it would be a mistake to lose you.
I want to be yours, but I'm not yours. I know I'm talking too much, but I want you to postpone taking the test.

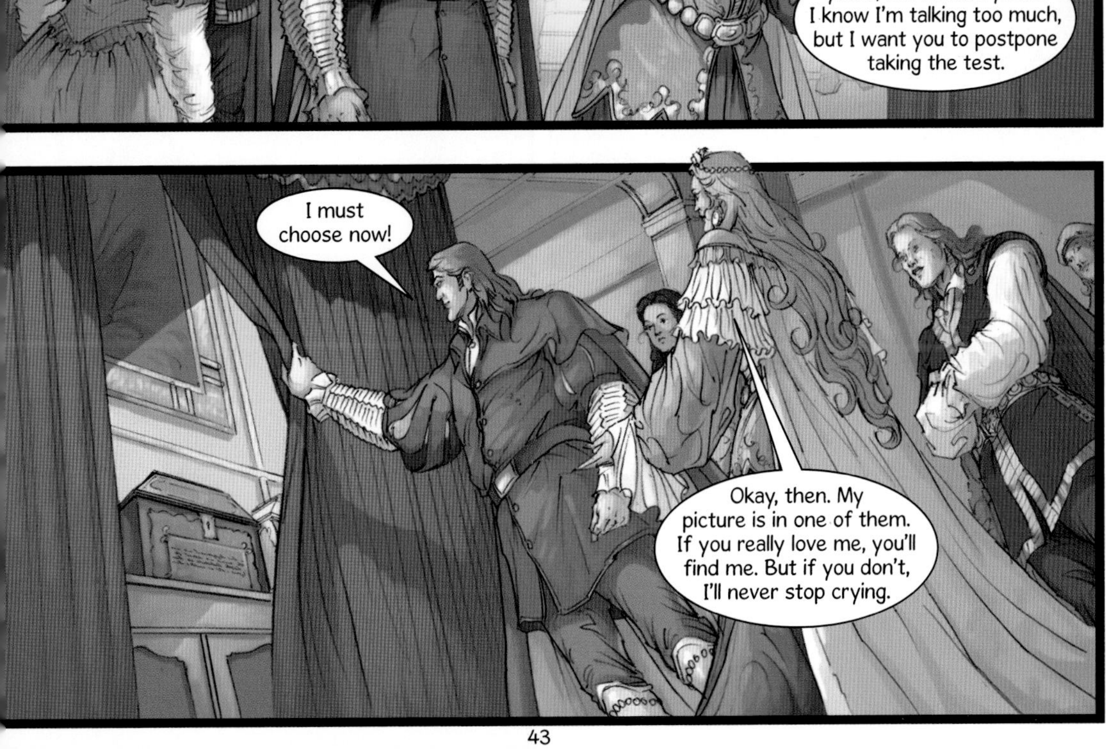
I must choose now!
Okay, then. My picture is in one of them. If you really love me, you'll find me. But if you don't, I'll never stop crying.

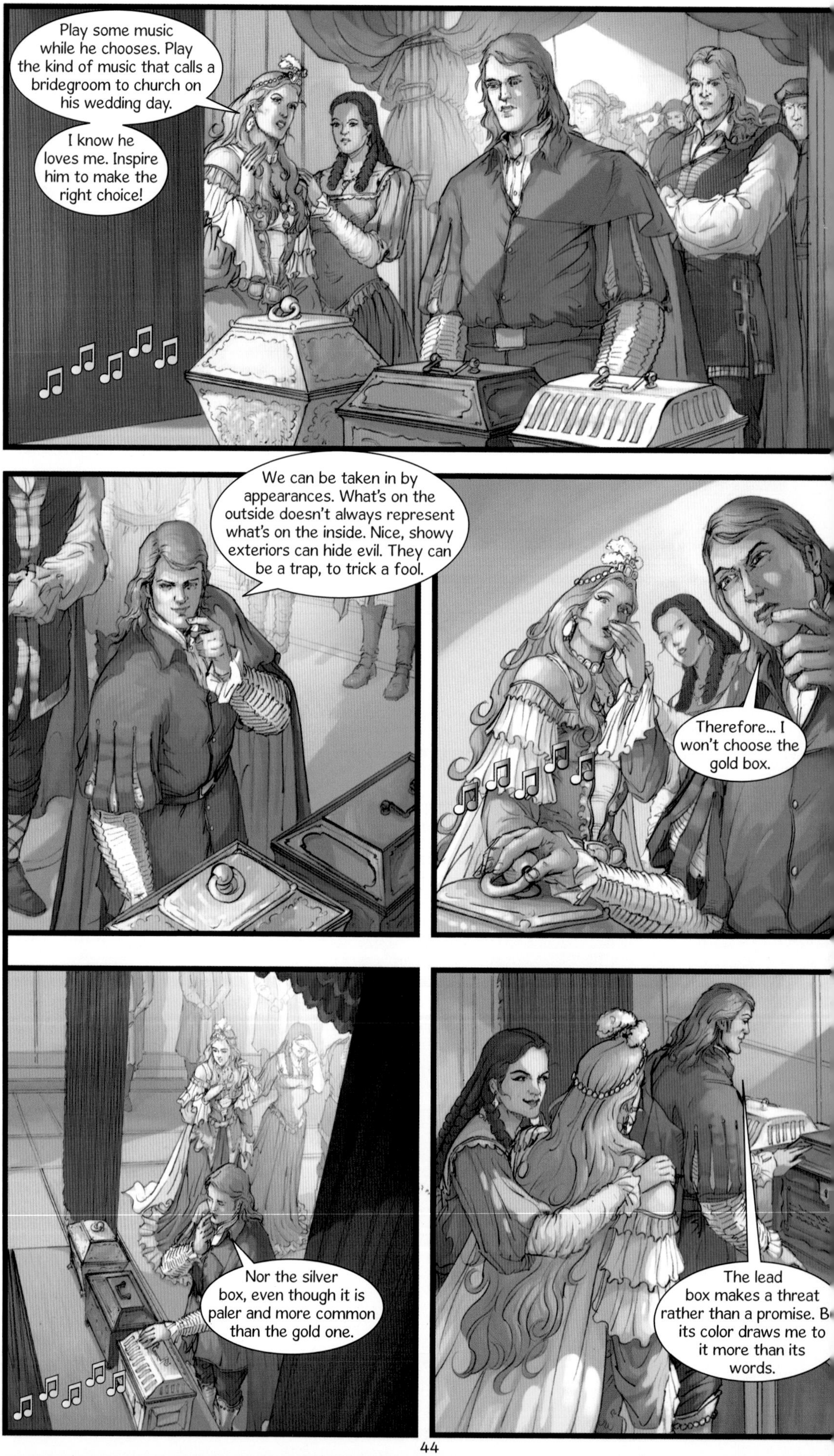
Play some music while he chooses. Play the kind of music that calls a bridegroom to church on his wedding day.
I know he loves me. Inspire him to make the right choice!
We can be taken in by appearances. What's on the outside doesn't always represent what's on the inside. Nice, showy exteriors can hide evil. They can be a trap, to trick a fool.
Therefore... I won't choose the gold box.
Nor the silver box, even though it is paler and more common than the gold one.
The lead box makes a threat rather than a promise. B
its color draws me to it more than its words.

The lead box is my choice. What will I find inside?

Oh... I'm so excited. All my doubts and fears are flying away!

I must stay calm. It's too intense. I need to control my emotions or I'll make myself sick.

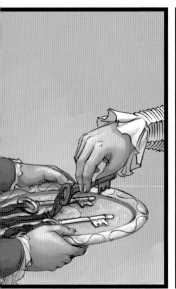

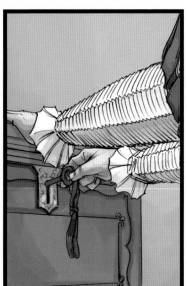

HOORAY

It's Portia's picture! And beautiful as it is, it's only a poor imitation of the real thing.

Let me read the scroll.

45

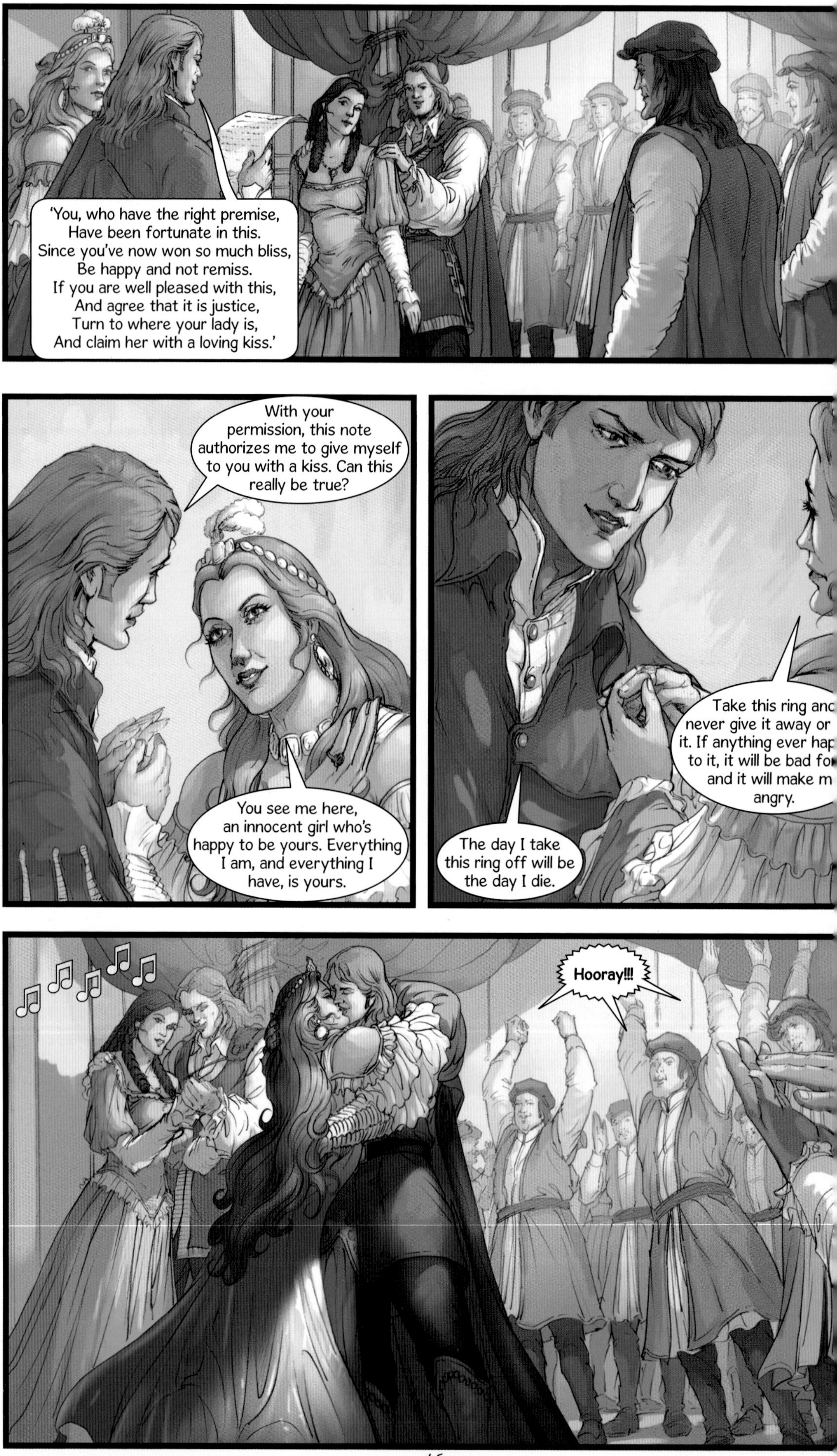
'You, who have the right premise, Have been fortunate in this. Since you've now won so much bliss, Be happy and not remiss. If you are well pleased with this, And agree that it is justice, Turn to where your lady is, And claim her with a loving kiss.'
With your permission, this note authorizes me to give myself to you with a kiss. Can this really be true?
You see me here, an innocent girl who's happy to be yours. Everything I am, and everything I have, is yours.
Take this ring an never give it away or it. If anything ever ha to it, it will be bad fo and it will make m angry.
The day I take this ring off will be the day I die.
Hooray!!!

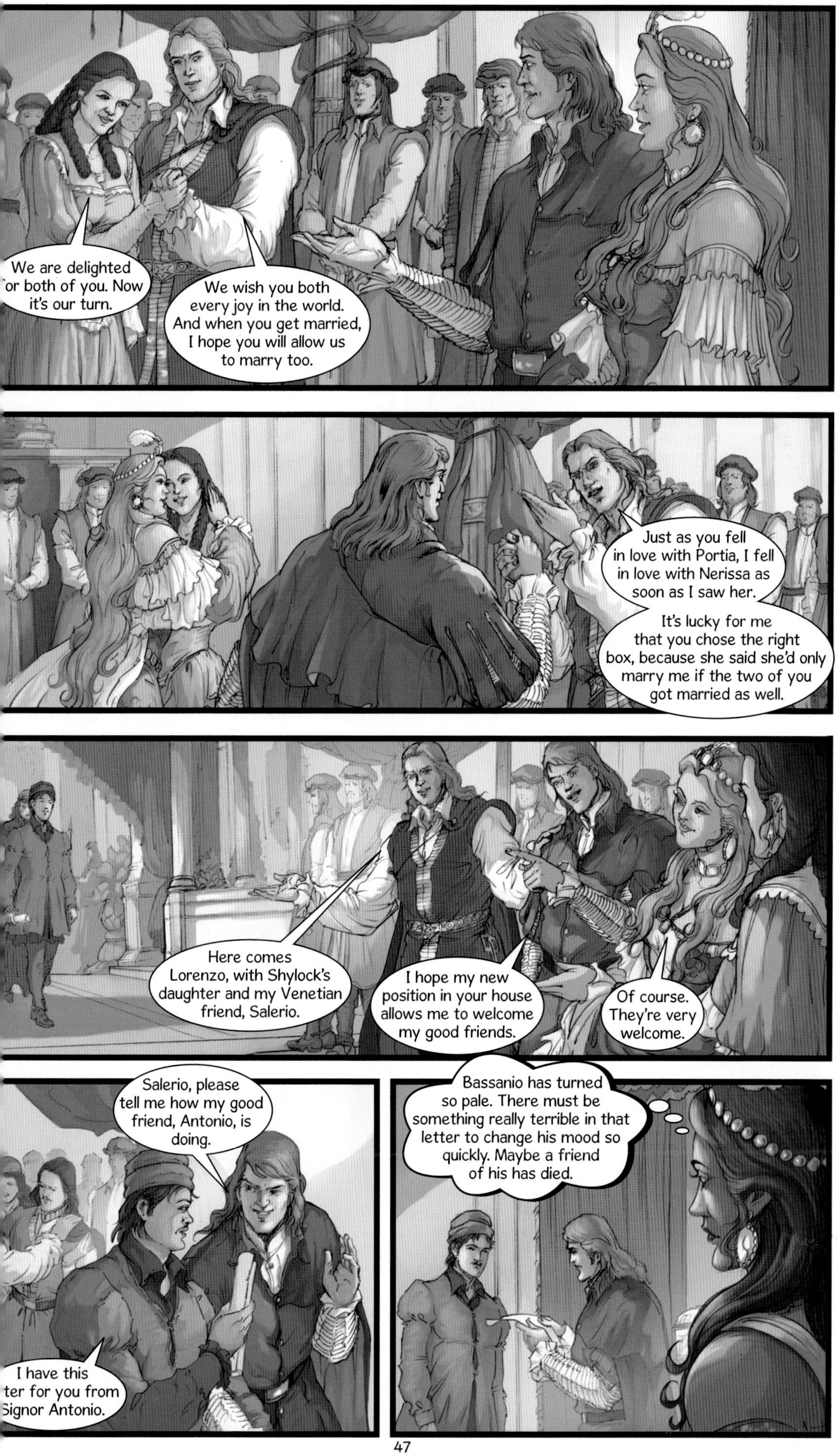
We are delighted or both of you. Now it's our turn.
We wish you both every joy in the world. And when you get married, I hope you will allow us to marry too.
Just as you fell in love with Portia, I fell in love with Nerissa as soon as I saw her.
It's lucky for me that you chose the right box, because she said she'd only marry me if the two of you got married as well.
Here comes Lorenzo, with Shylock's daughter and my Venetian friend, Salerio.
I hope my new position in your house allows me to welcome my good friends.
Of course. They're very welcome.
Salerio, please tell me how my good friend, Antonio, is doing.
I have this ter for you from Signor Antonio.
Bassanio has turned so pale. There must be something really terrible in that letter to change his mood so quickly. Maybe a friend of his has died.

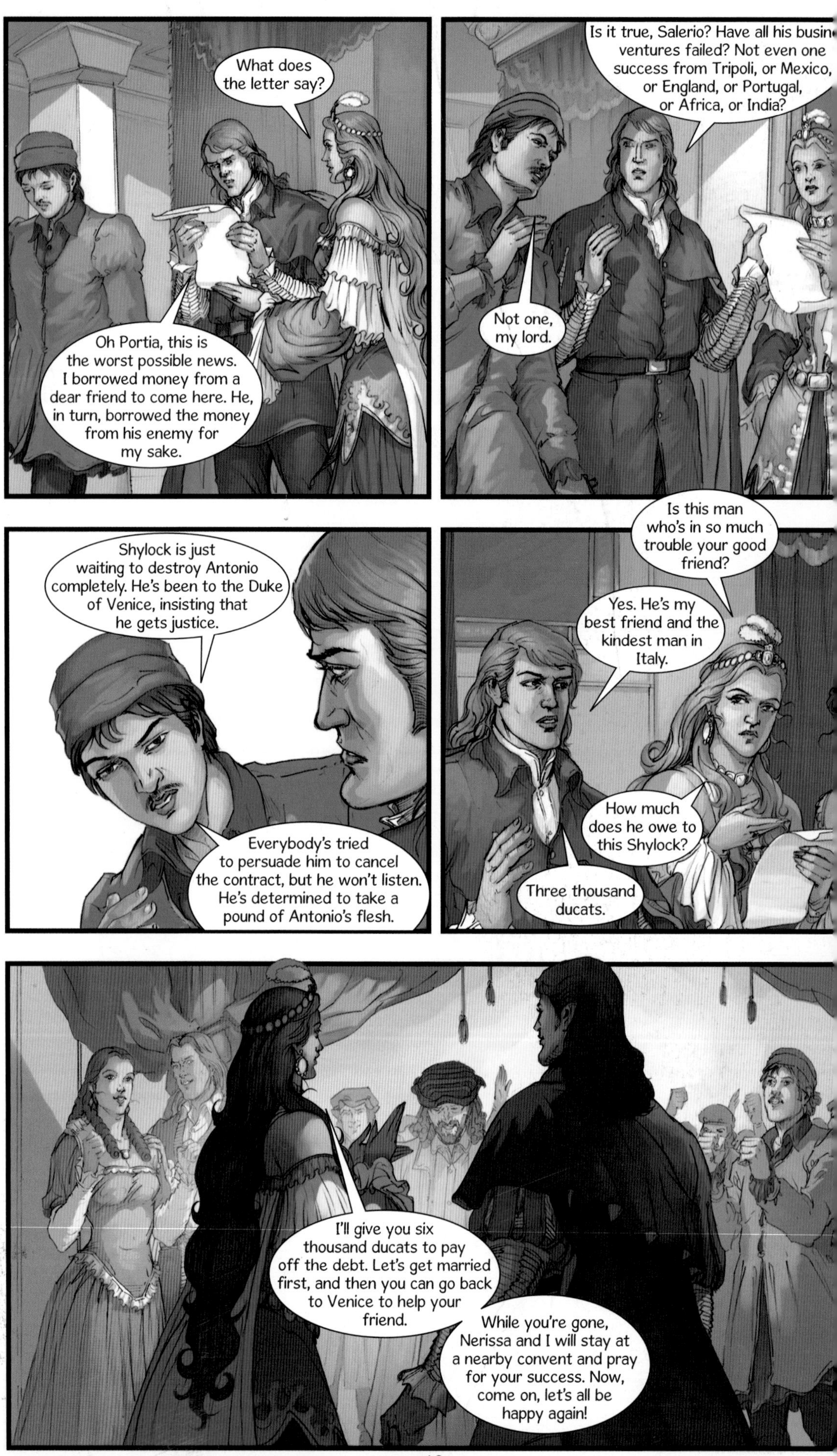
What does the letter say?
Oh Portia, this is the worst possible news. I borrowed money from a dear friend to come here. He, in turn, borrowed the money from his enemy for my sake.
Is it true, Salerio? Have all his busin
ventures failed? Not even one success from Tripoli, or Mexico, or England, or Portugal, or Africa, or India?
Not one, my lord.
Shylock is just waiting to destroy Antonio completely. He's been to the Duke of Venice, insisting that he gets justice.
Everybody's tried to persuade him to cancel the contract, but he won't listen. He's determined to take a pound of Antonio's flesh.
Is this man who's in so much trouble your good friend?
Yes. He's my best friend and the kindest man in Italy.
How much does he owe to this Shylock?
Three thousand ducats.
I'll give you six thousand ducats to pay off the debt. Let's get married first, and then you can go back to Venice to help your friend.
While you're gone, Nerissa and I will stay at a nearby convent and pray for your success. Now, come on, let's all be happy again!

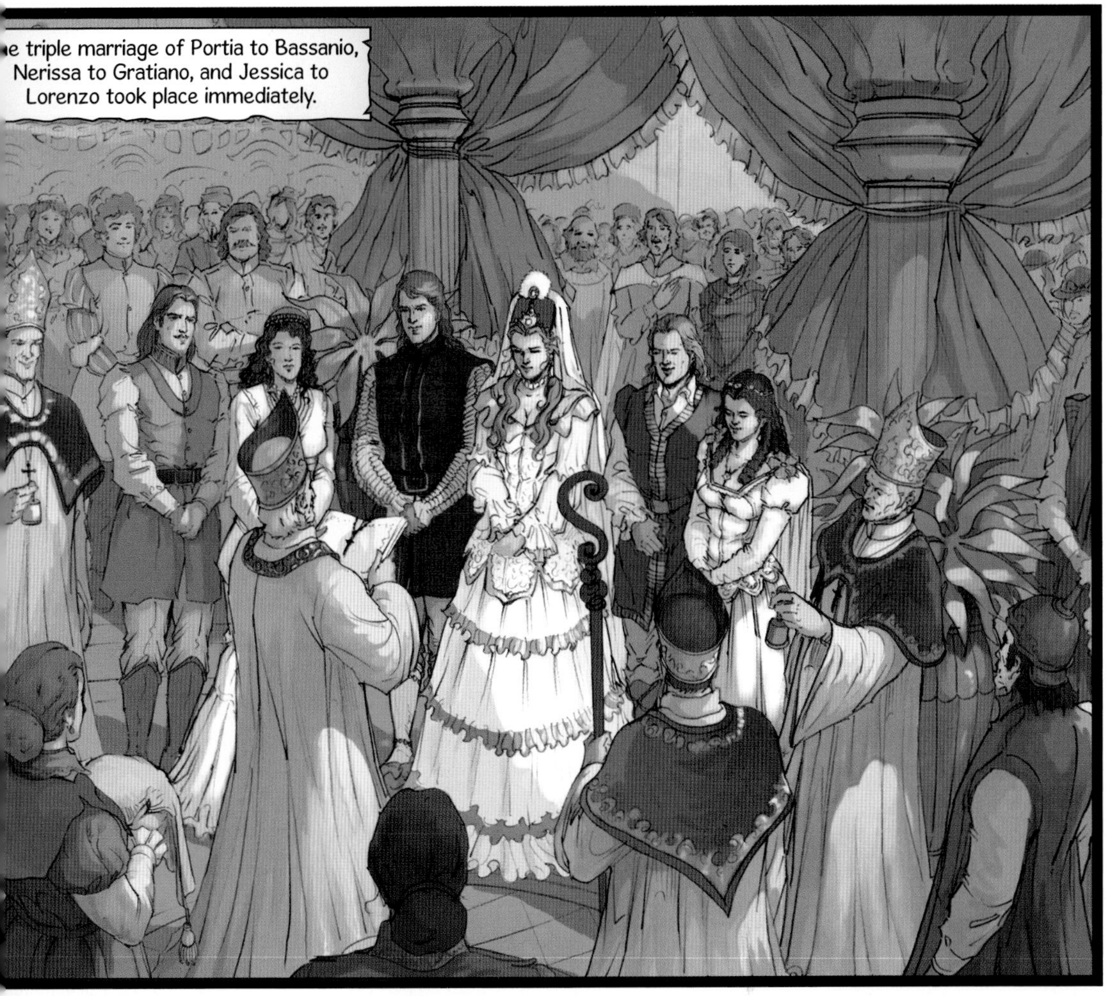
e triple marriage of Portia to Bassanio, Nerissa to Gratiano, and Jessica to Lorenzo took place immediately.

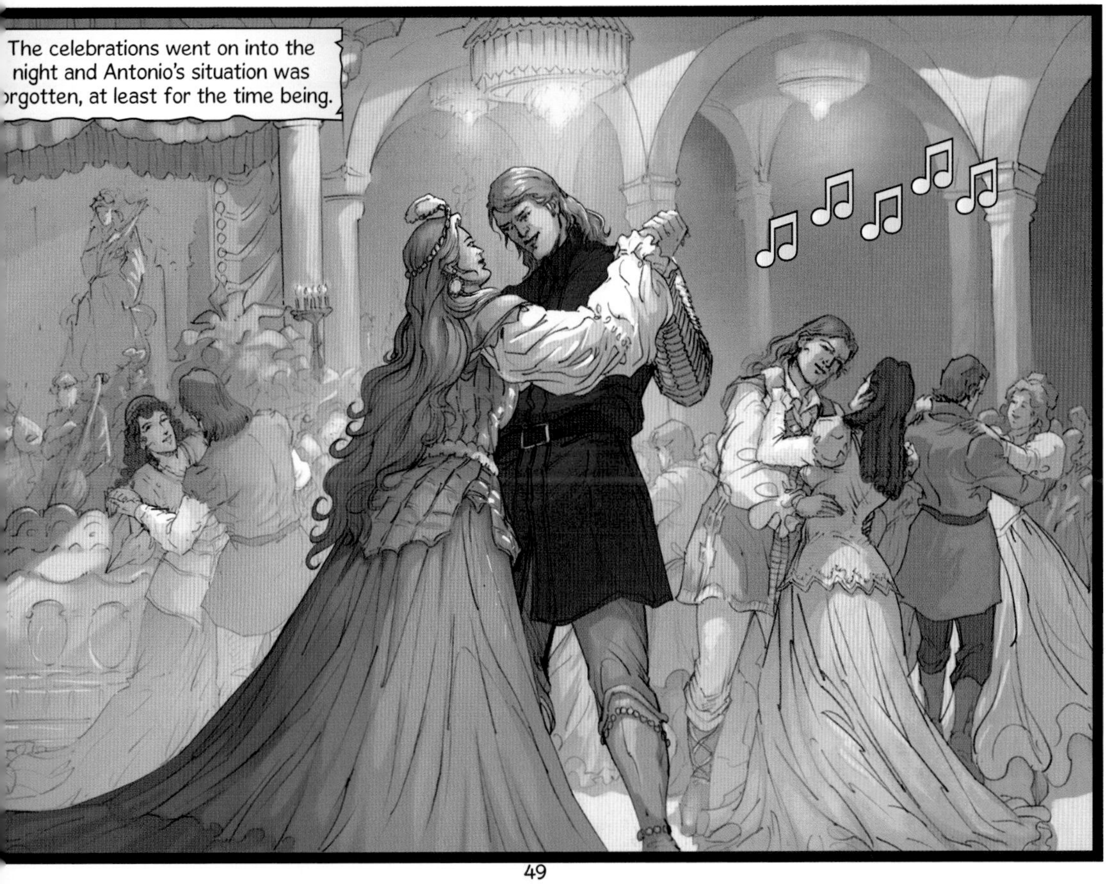
The celebrations went on into the night and Antonio's situation was rgotten, at least for the time being.

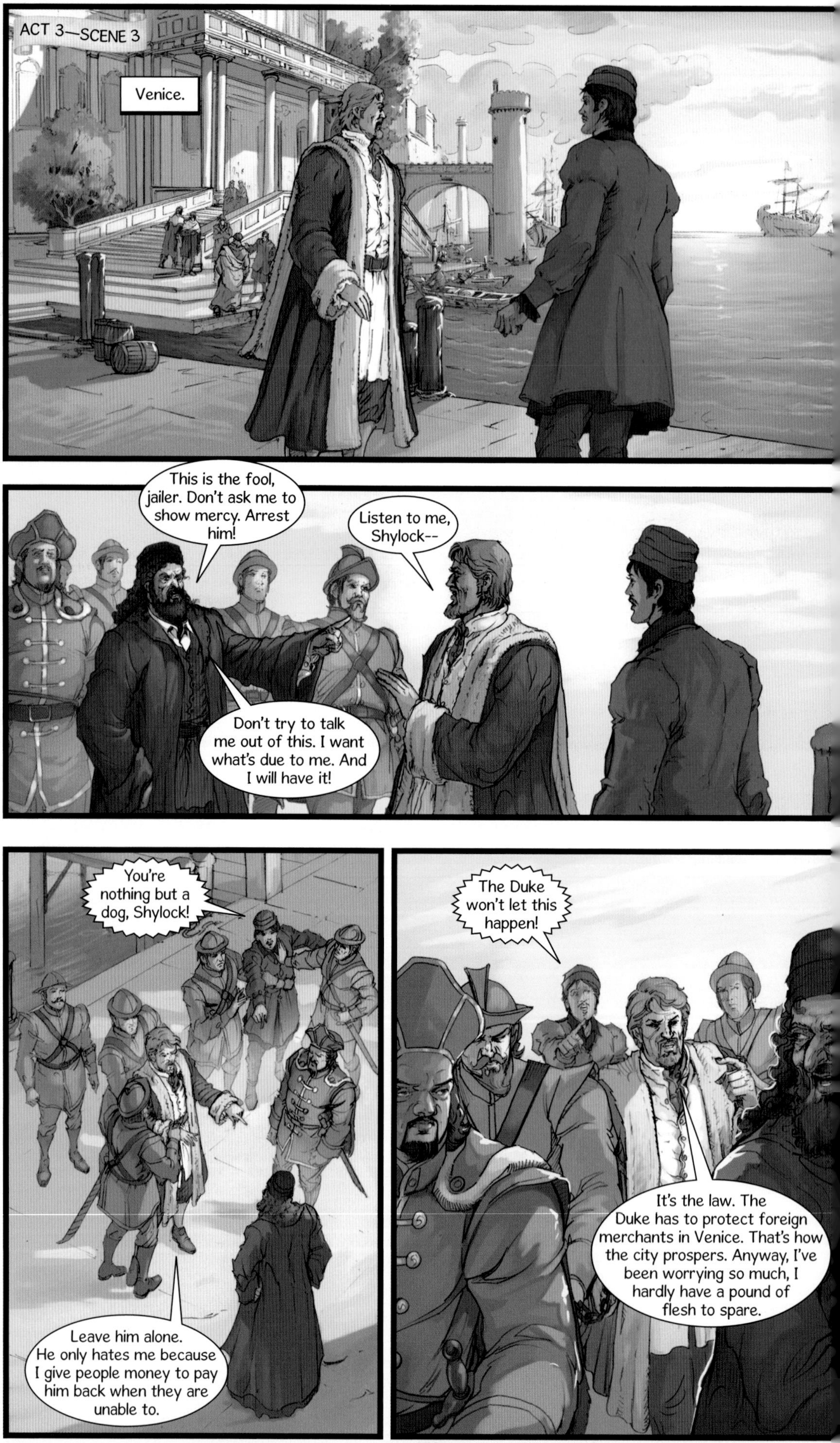
ACT 3—SCENE 3
Venice.
This is the fool, jailer. Don't ask me to show mercy. Arrest him!
Listen to me, Shylock--
Don't try to talk me out of this. I want what's due to me. And I will have it!
You're nothing but a dog, Shylock!
Leave him alone. He only hates me because I give people money to pay him back when they are unable to.
The Duke won't let this happen!
It's the law. The Duke has to protect foreign merchants in Venice. That's how the city prospers. Anyway, I've been worrying so much, I hardly have a pound of flesh to spare.

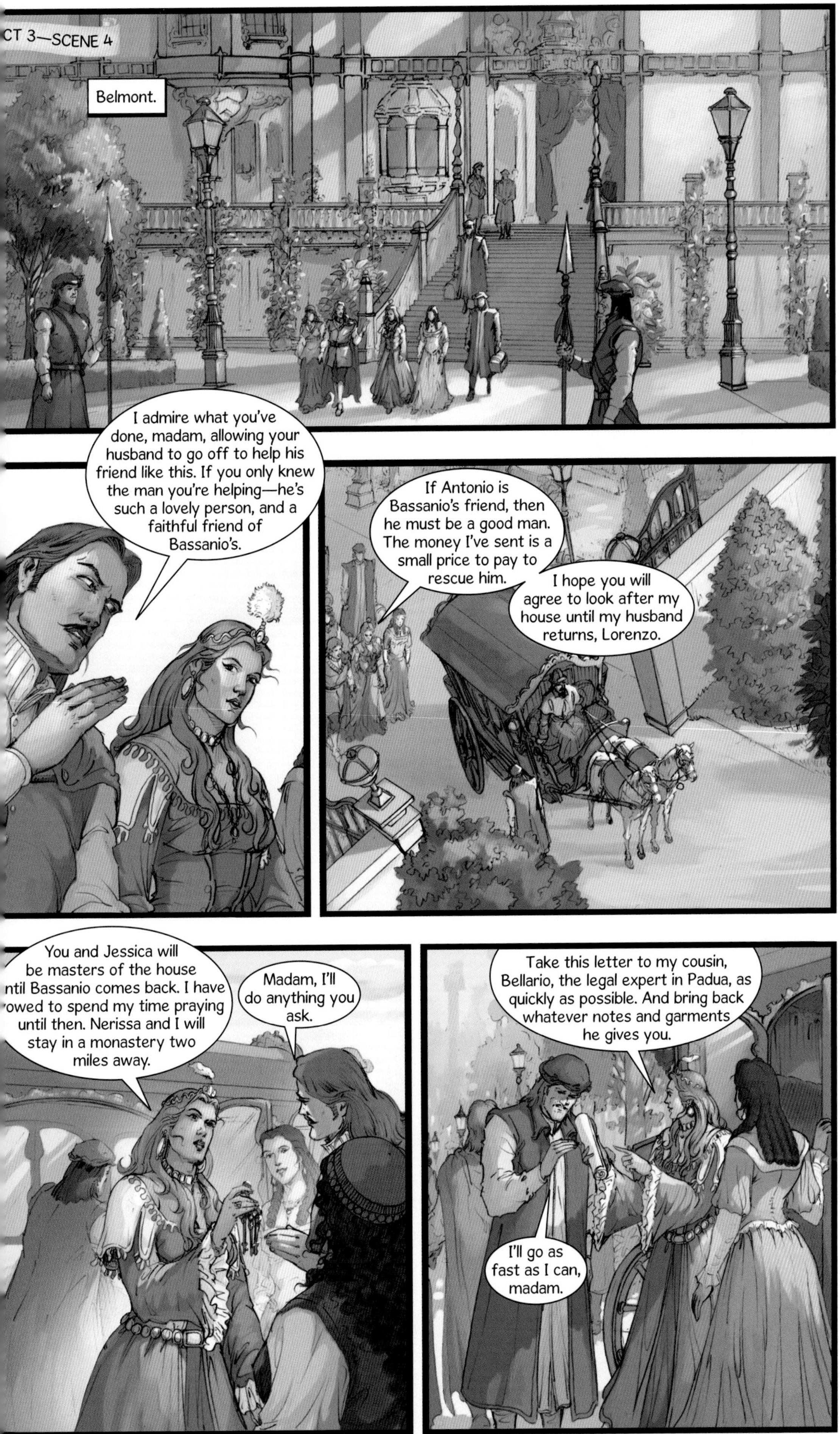
CT 3—SCENE 4
Belmont.
I admire what you've done, madam, allowing your husband to go off to help his friend like this. If you only knew the man you're helping—he's such a lovely person, and a faithful friend of Bassanio's.
If Antonio is Bassanio's friend, then he must be a good man. The money I've sent is a small price to pay to rescue him.
I hope you will agree to look after my house until my husband returns, Lorenzo.
You and Jessica will be masters of the house ntil Bassanio comes back. I have owed to spend my time praying until then. Nerissa and I will stay in a monastery two miles away.
Madam, I'll do anything you ask.
Take this letter to my cousin, Bellario, the legal expert in Padua, as quickly as possible. And bring back whatever notes and garments he gives you.
I'll go as fast as I can, madam.

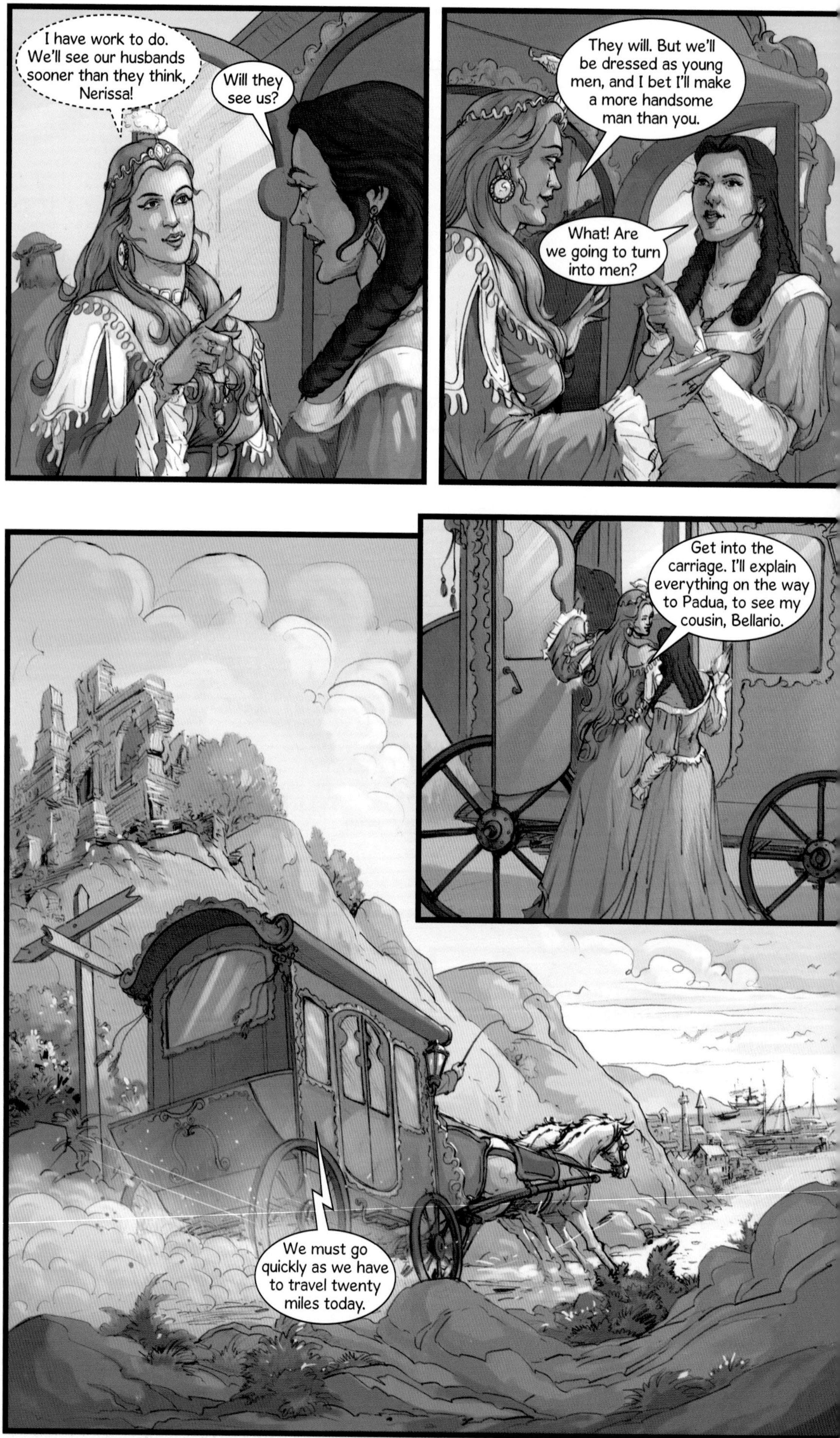

I have work to do. We'll see our husbands sooner than they think, Nerissa!
Will they see us?
They will. But we'll be dressed as young men, and I bet I'll make a more handsome man than you.
What! Are we going to turn into men?
Get into the carriage. I'll explain everything on the way to Padua, to see my cousin, Bellario.
We must go quickly as we have to travel twenty miles today.

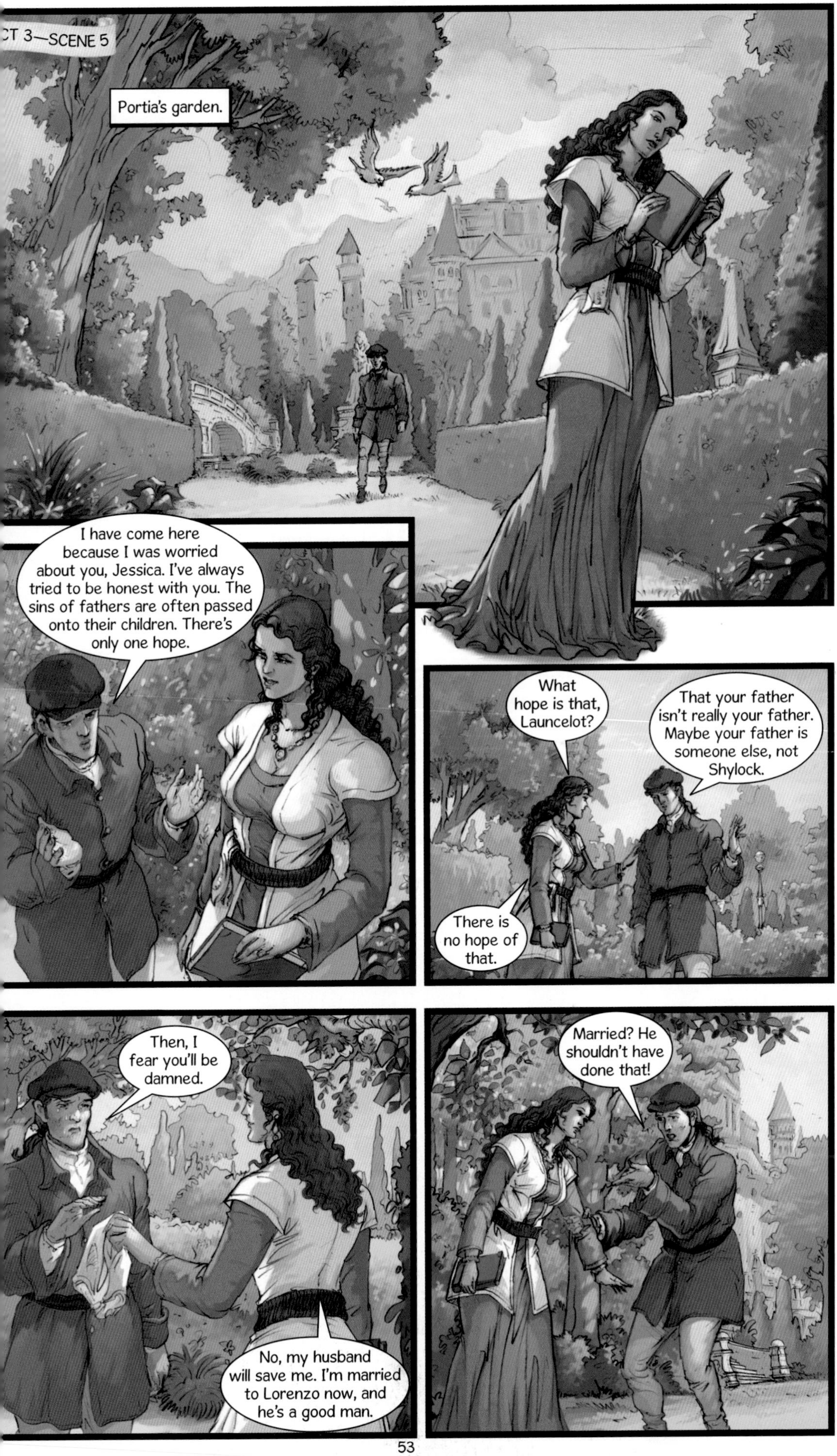

ACT 3—SCENE 5
Portia's garden.
I have come here because I was worried about you, Jessica. I've always tried to be honest with you. The sins of fathers are often passed onto their children. There's only one hope.
What hope is that, Launcelot?
That your father isn't really your father. Maybe your father is someone else, not Shylock.
There is no hope of that.
Then, I fear you'll be damned.
No, my husband will save me. I'm married to Lorenzo now, and he's a good man.
Married? He shouldn't have done that!

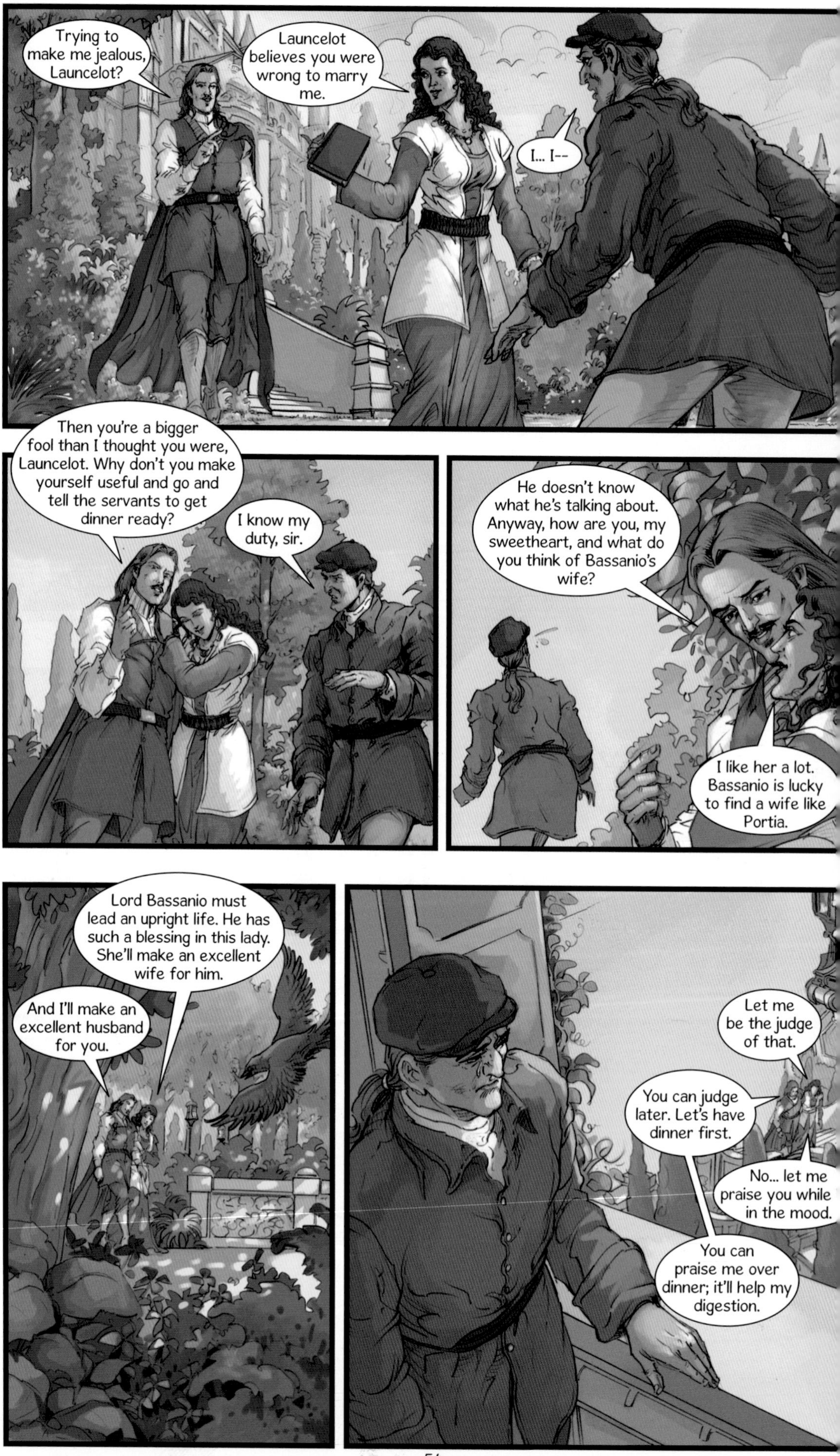
Trying to make me jealous, Launcelot?
Launcelot believes you were wrong to marry me.
I... I--
Then you're a bigger fool than I thought you were, Launcelot. Why don't you make yourself useful and go and tell the servants to get dinner ready?
I know my duty, sir.
He doesn't know what he's talking about. Anyway, how are you, my sweetheart, and what do you think of Bassanio's wife?
I like her a lot. Bassanio is lucky to find a wife like Portia.
Lord Bassanio must lead an upright life. He has such a blessing in this lady. She'll make an excellent wife for him.
And I'll make an excellent husband for you.
Let me be the judge of that.
You can judge later. Let's have dinner first.
No... let me praise you while in the mood.
You can praise me over dinner; it'll help my digestion.

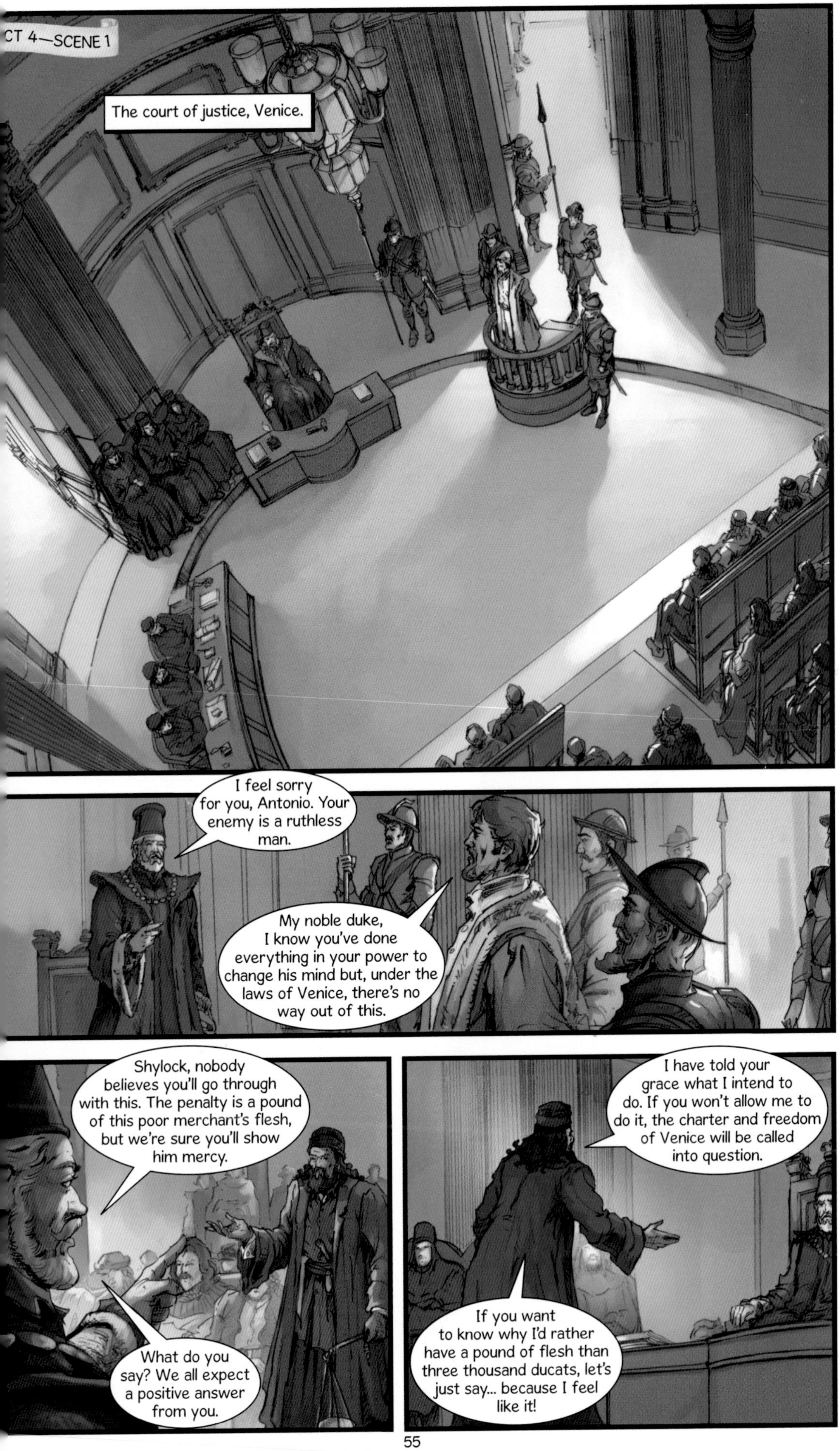
CT 4—SCENE 1
The court of justice, Venice.
I feel sorry for you, Antonio. Your enemy is a ruthless man.
My noble duke, I know you've done everything in your power to change his mind but, under the laws of Venice, there's no way out of this.
Shylock, nobody believes you'll go through with this. The penalty is a pound of this poor merchant's flesh, but we're sure you'll show him mercy.
What do you say? We all expect a positive answer from you.
I have told your grace what I intend to do. If you won't allow me to do it, the charter and freedom of Venice will be called into question.
If you want to know why I'd rather have a pound of flesh than three thousand ducats, let's just say... because I feel like it!

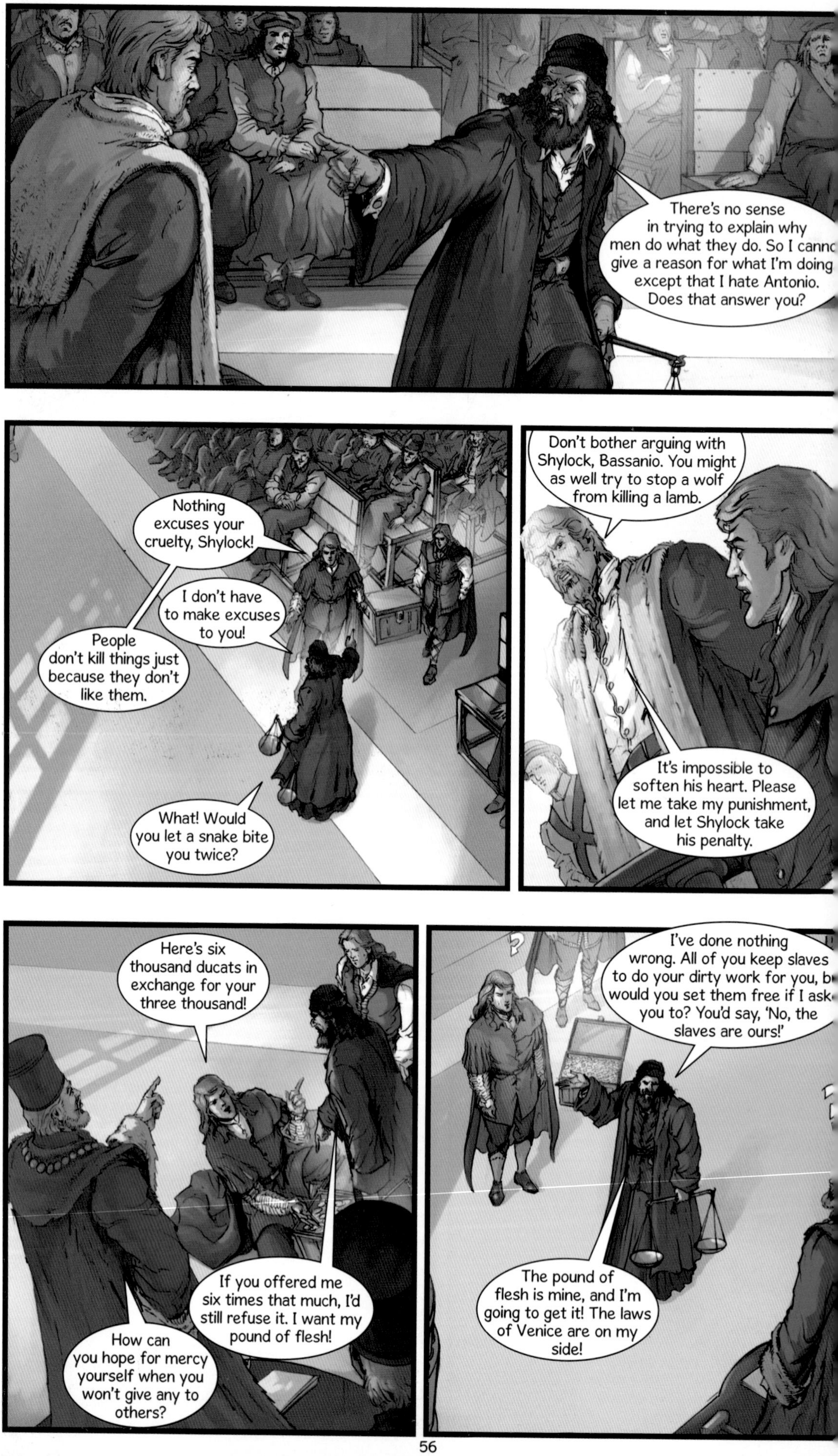
There's no sense in trying to explain why men do what they do. So I canno give a reason for what I'm doing except that I hate Antonio. Does that answer you?
Nothing excuses your cruelty, Shylock!
I don't have to make excuses to you!
People don't kill things just because they don't like them.
What! Would you let a snake bite you twice?
Don't bother arguing with Shylock, Bassanio. You might as well try to stop a wolf from killing a lamb.
It's impossible to soften his heart. Please let me take my punishment, and let Shylock take his penalty.
Here's six thousand ducats in exchange for your three thousand!
If you offered me six times that much, I'd still refuse it. I want my pound of flesh!
How can you hope for mercy yourself when you won't give any to others?
I've done nothing wrong. All of you keep slaves to do your dirty work for you, b would you set them free if I ask you to? You'd say, 'No, the slaves are ours!'
The pound of flesh is mine, and I'm going to get it! The laws of Venice are on my side!

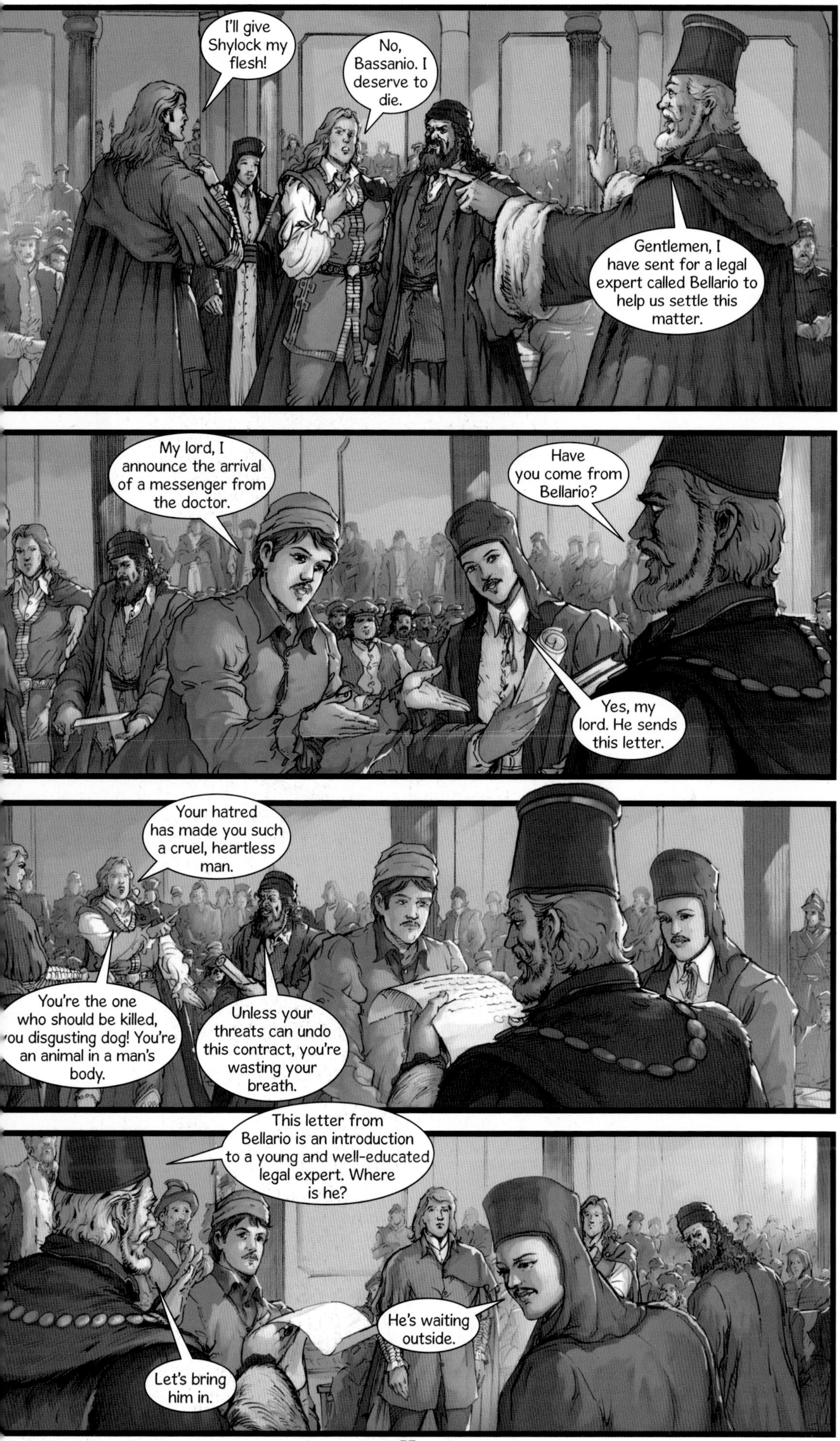
I'll give Shylock my flesh!
No, Bassanio. I deserve to die.
Gentlemen, I have sent for a legal expert called Bellario to help us settle this matter.
My lord, I announce the arrival of a messenger from the doctor.
Have you come from Bellario?
Yes, my lord. He sends this letter.
Your hatred has made you such a cruel, heartless man.
You're the one who should be killed, ou disgusting dog! You're an animal in a man's body.
Unless your threats can undo this contract, you're wasting your breath.
This letter from Bellario is an introduction to a young and well-educated legal expert. Where is he?
He's waiting outside.
Let's bring him in.

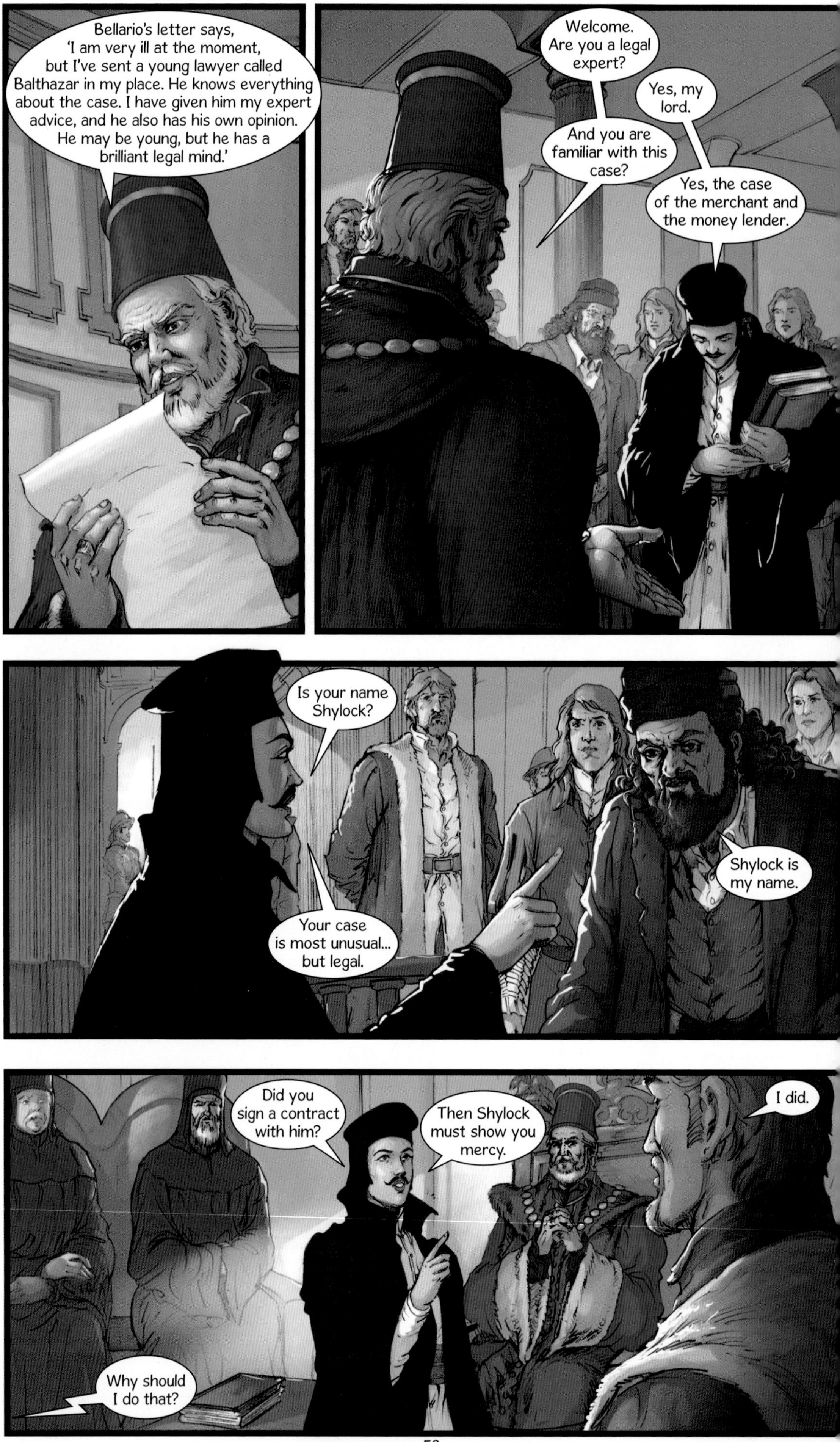
Bellario's letter says, 'I am very ill at the moment, but I've sent a young lawyer called Balthazar in my place. He knows everything about the case. I have given him my expert advice, and he also has his own opinion. He may be young, but he has a brilliant legal mind.'
Welcome. Are you a legal expert?
Yes, my lord.
And you are familiar with this case?
Yes, the case of the merchant and the money lender.
Is your name Shylock?
Shylock is my name.
Your case is most unusual... but legal.
Did you sign a contract with him?
I did.
Then Shylock must show you mercy.
Why should I do that?

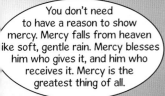

You don't need to have a reason to show mercy. Mercy falls from heaven like soft, gentle rain. Mercy blesses him who gives it, and him who receives it. Mercy is the greatest thing of all.

Mercy makes a king look better than any crown or scepter can. Mercy is a quality given to us by God, and we are closest to God when we show it.

So, Shylock, even though the law is on your side, the law won't save your soul. I'm asking you to give up your case.

But if you don't, the laws of Venice will ensure the sentence is carried out against this merchant here.

I take full responsibility for my decision. I want the law, the penalty, and what was agreed in my contract.

And here I am, offering to pay back twice the amount in the contract. If that's not enough, I'll agree to pay back ten times as much.

You can take my hands, my head, my heart as security. If that's not enough, then it seems evil is stronger than truth.

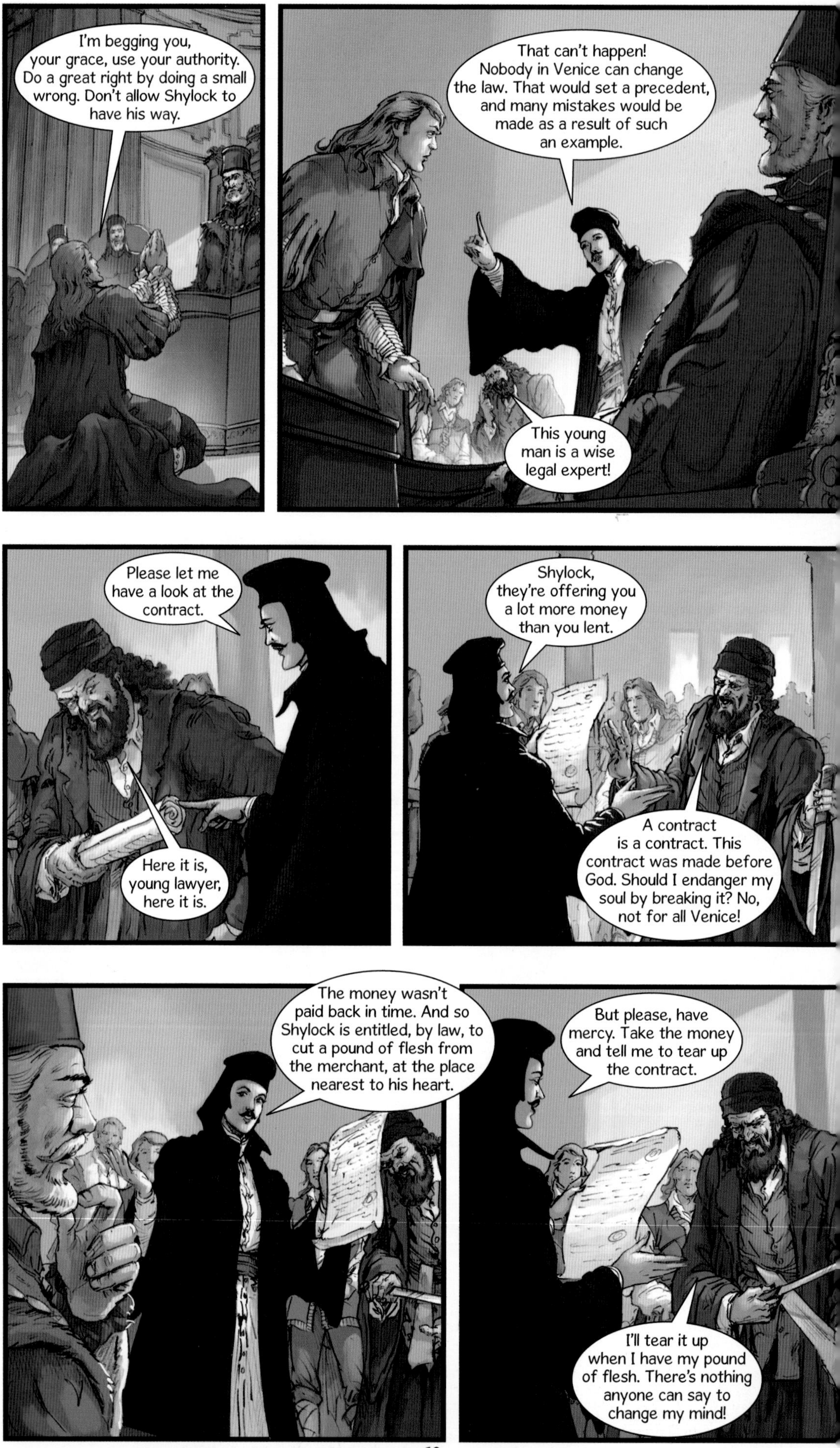
I'm begging you, your grace, use your authority. Do a great right by doing a small wrong. Don't allow Shylock to have his way.
That can't happen! Nobody in Venice can change the law. That would set a precedent, and many mistakes would be made as a result of such an example.
This young man is a wise legal expert!
Please let me have a look at the contract.
Here it is, young lawyer, here it is.
Shylock, they're offering you a lot more money than you lent.
A contract is a contract. This contract was made before God. Should I endanger my soul by breaking it? No, not for all Venice!
The money wasn't paid back in time. And so Shylock is entitled, by law, to cut a pound of flesh from the merchant, at the place nearest to his heart.
But please, have mercy. Take the money and tell me to tear up the contract.
I'll tear it up when I have my pound of flesh. There's nothing anyone can say to change my mind!

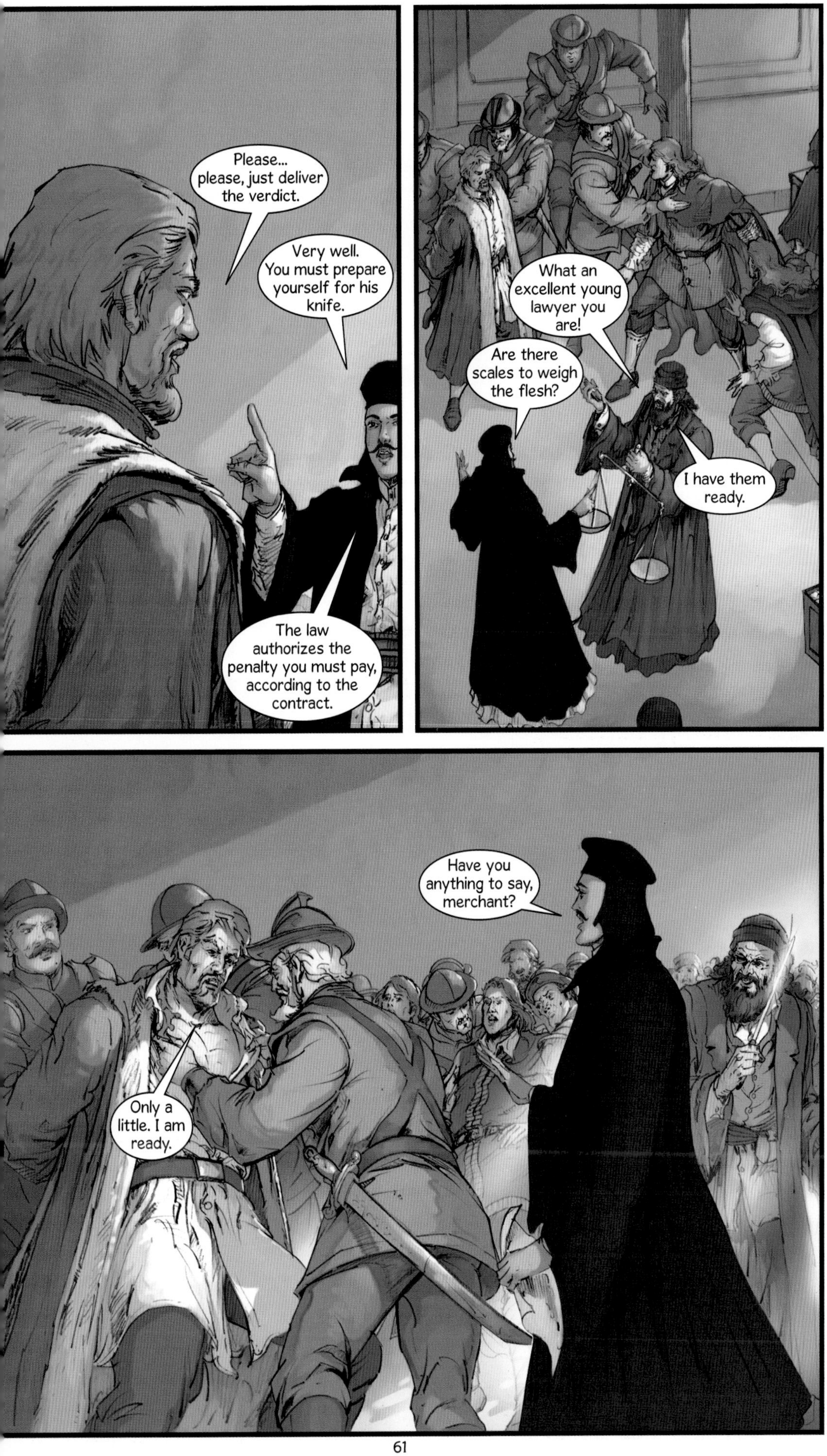
Please... please, just deliver the verdict.
Very well. You must prepare yourself for his knife.
The law authorizes the penalty you must pay, according to the contract.
What an excellent young lawyer you are!
Are there scales to weigh the flesh?
I have them ready.
Have you anything to say, merchant?
Only a little. I am ready.

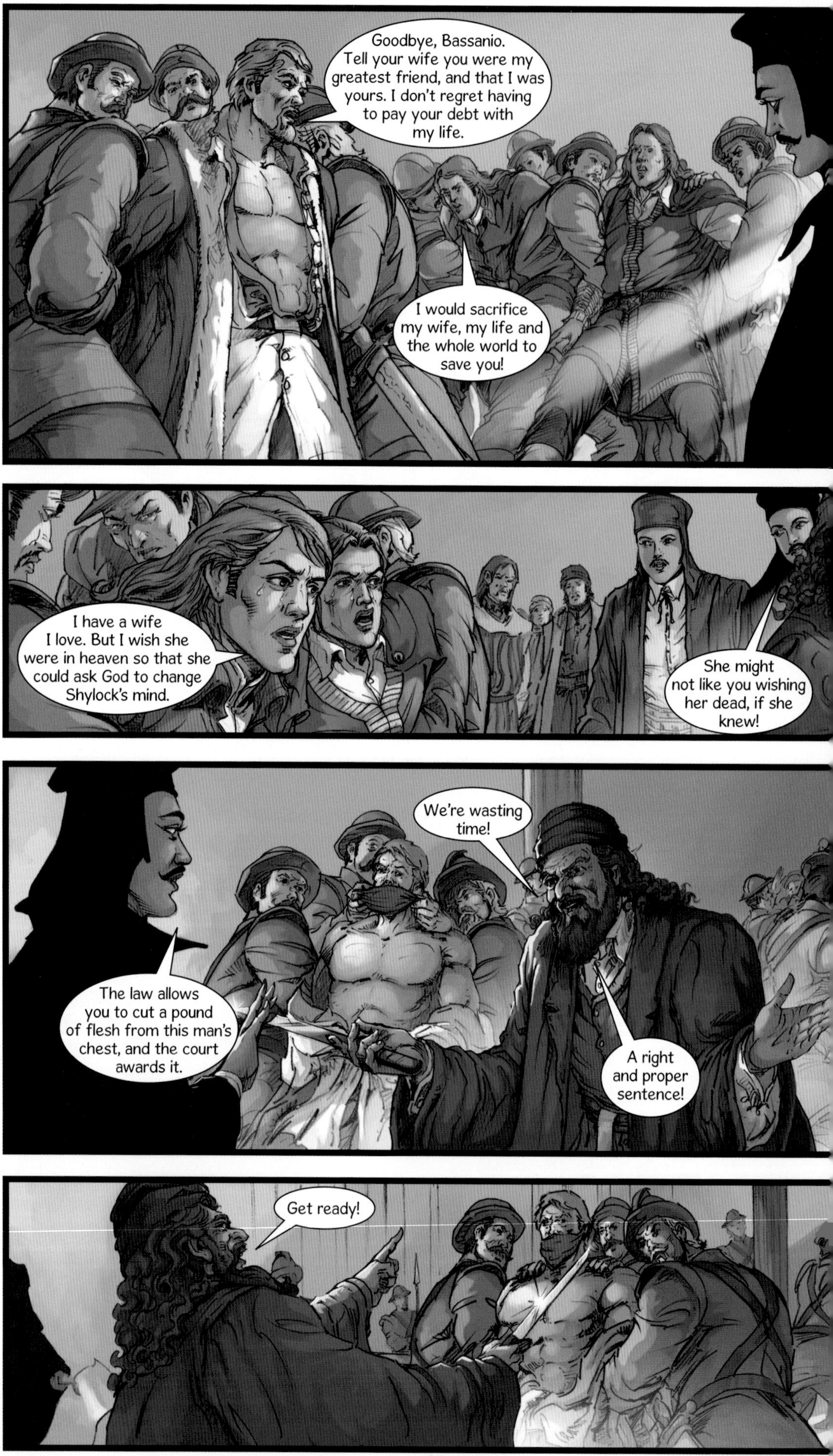
Goodbye, Bassanio. Tell your wife you were my greatest friend, and that I was yours. I don't regret having to pay your debt with my life.
I would sacrifice my wife, my life and the whole world to save you!
I have a wife I love. But I wish she were in heaven so that she could ask God to change Shylock's mind.
She might not like you wishing her dead, if she knew!
We're wasting time!
The law allows you to cut a pound of flesh from this man's chest, and the court awards it.
A right and proper sentence!
Get ready!

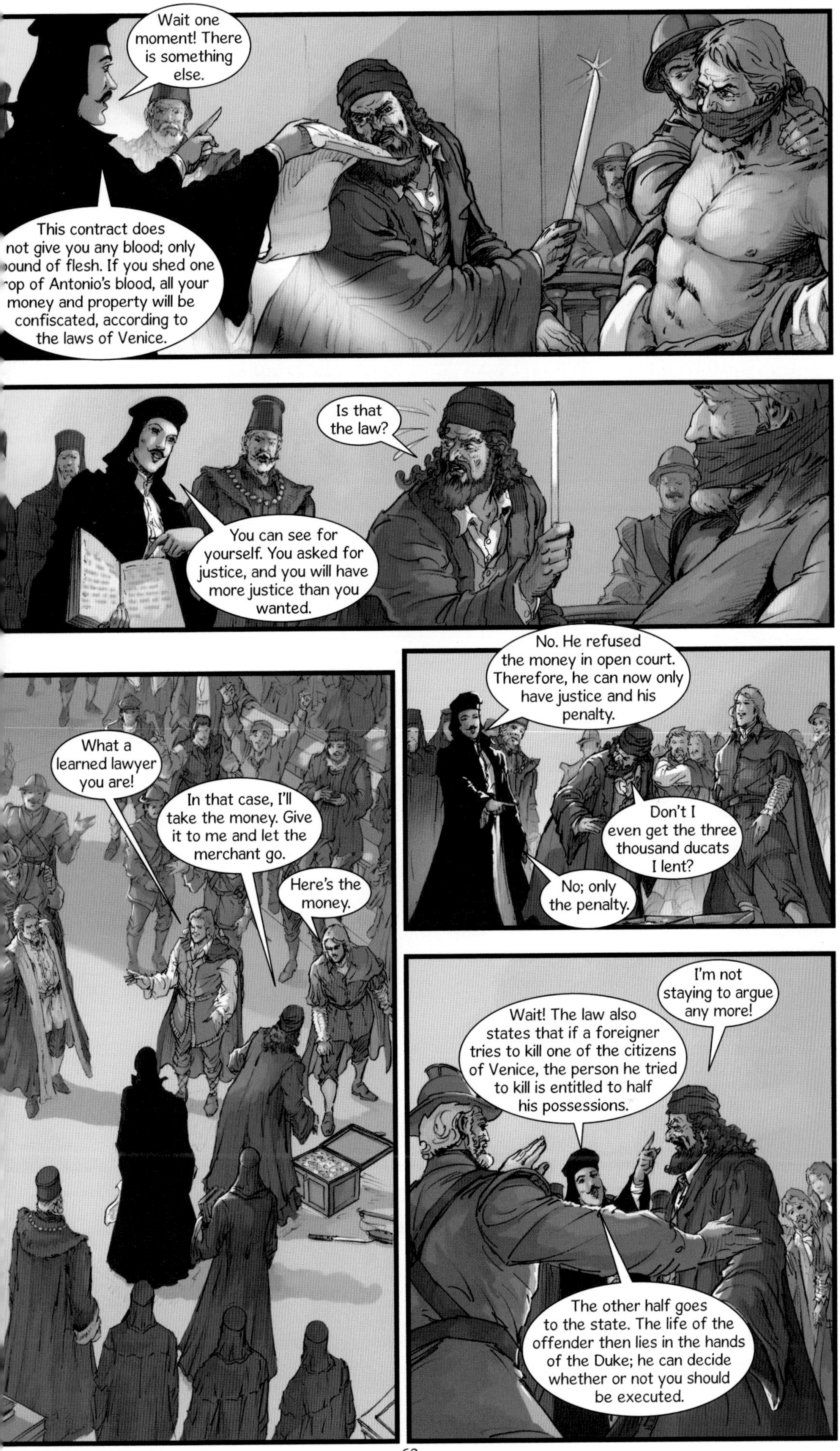
Wait one moment! There is something else.
This contract does not give you any blood; only ›ound of flesh. If you shed one ›op of Antonio's blood, all your money and property will be confiscated, according to the laws of Venice.
Is that the law?
You can see for yourself. You asked for justice, and you will have more justice than you wanted.
What a learned lawyer you are!
In that case, I'll take the money. Give it to me and let the merchant go.
Here's the money.
No. He refused the money in open court. Therefore, he can now only have justice and his penalty.
Don't I even get the three thousand ducats I lent?
No; only the penalty.
I'm not staying to argue any more!
Wait! The law also states that if a foreigner tries to kill one of the citizens of Venice, the person he tried to kill is entitled to half his possessions.
The other half goes to the state. The life of the offender then lies in the hands of the Duke; he can decide whether or not you should be executed.

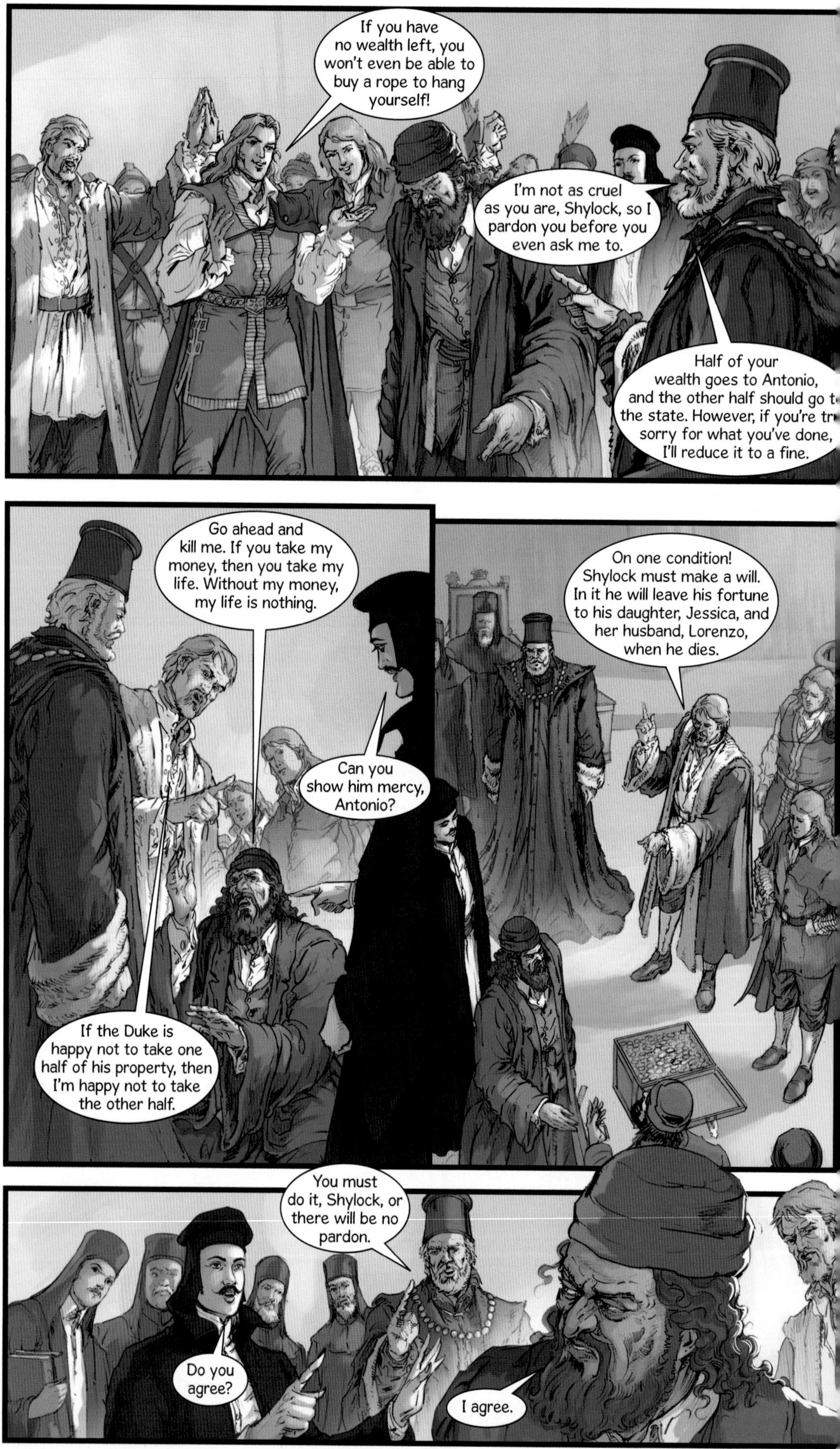
If you have no wealth left, you won't even be able to buy a rope to hang yourself!
I'm not as cruel as you are, Shylock, so I pardon you before you even ask me to.
Half of your wealth goes to Antonio, and the other half should go t the state. However, if you're tr sorry for what you've done, I'll reduce it to a fine.
Go ahead and kill me. If you take my money, then you take my life. Without my money, my life is nothing.
Can you show him mercy, Antonio?
If the Duke is happy not to take one half of his property, then I'm happy not to take the other half.
On one condition! Shylock must make a will. In it he will leave his fortune to his daughter, Jessica, and her husband, Lorenzo, when he dies.
You must do it, Shylock, or there will be no pardon.
Do you agree?
I agree.

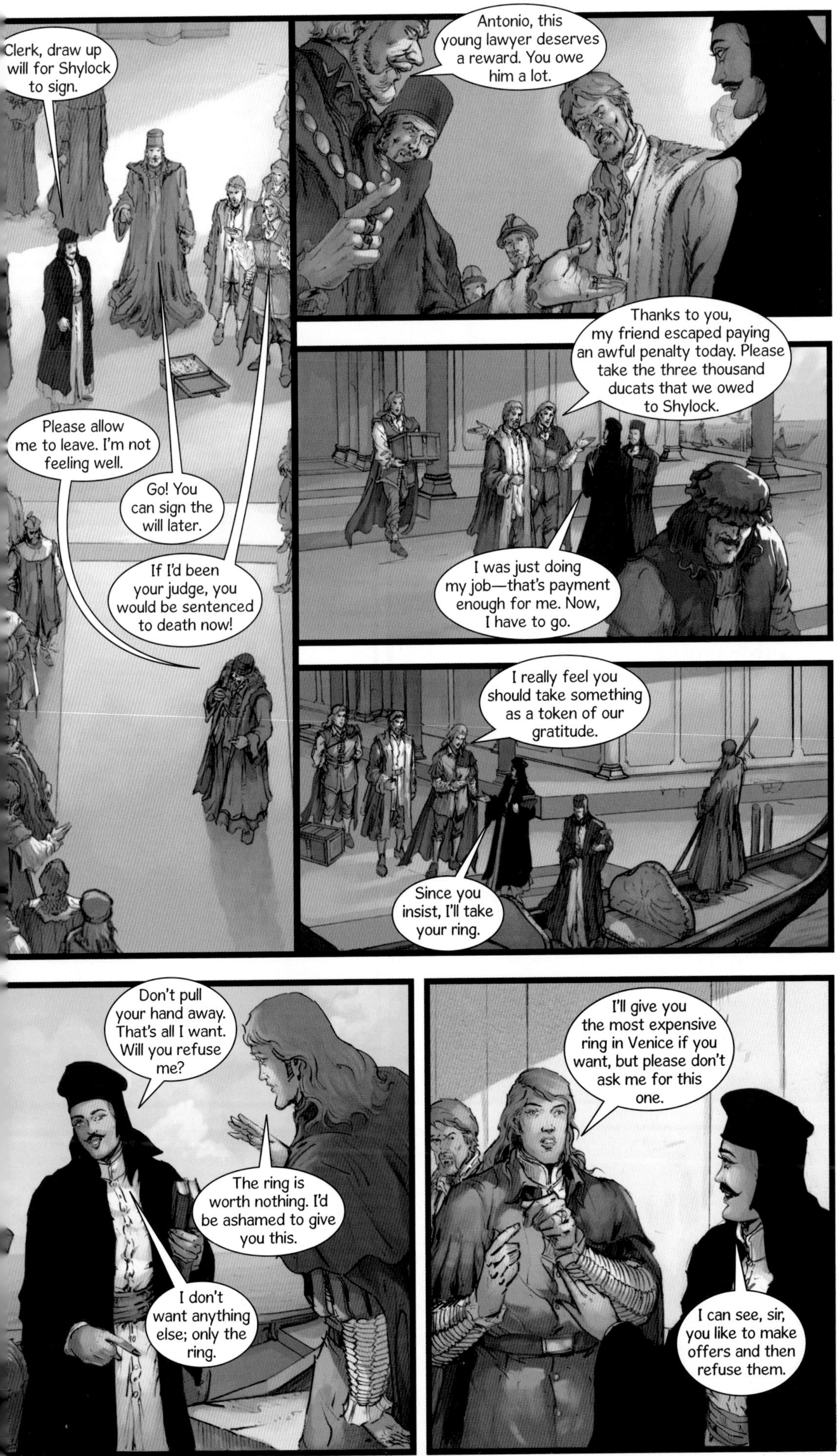
Clerk, draw up will for Shylock to sign.
Please allow me to leave. I'm not feeling well.
Go! You can sign the will later.
If I'd been your judge, you would be sentenced to death now!
Antonio, this young lawyer deserves a reward. You owe him a lot.
Thanks to you, my friend escaped paying an awful penalty today. Please take the three thousand ducats that we owed to Shylock.
I was just doing my job—that's payment enough for me. Now, I have to go.
I really feel you should take something as a token of our gratitude.
Since you insist, I'll take your ring.
Don't pull your hand away. That's all I want. Will you refuse me?
The ring is worth nothing. I'd be ashamed to give you this.
I don't want anything else; only the ring.
I'll give you the most expensive ring in Venice if you want, but please don't ask me for this one.
I can see, sir, you like to make offers and then refuse them.

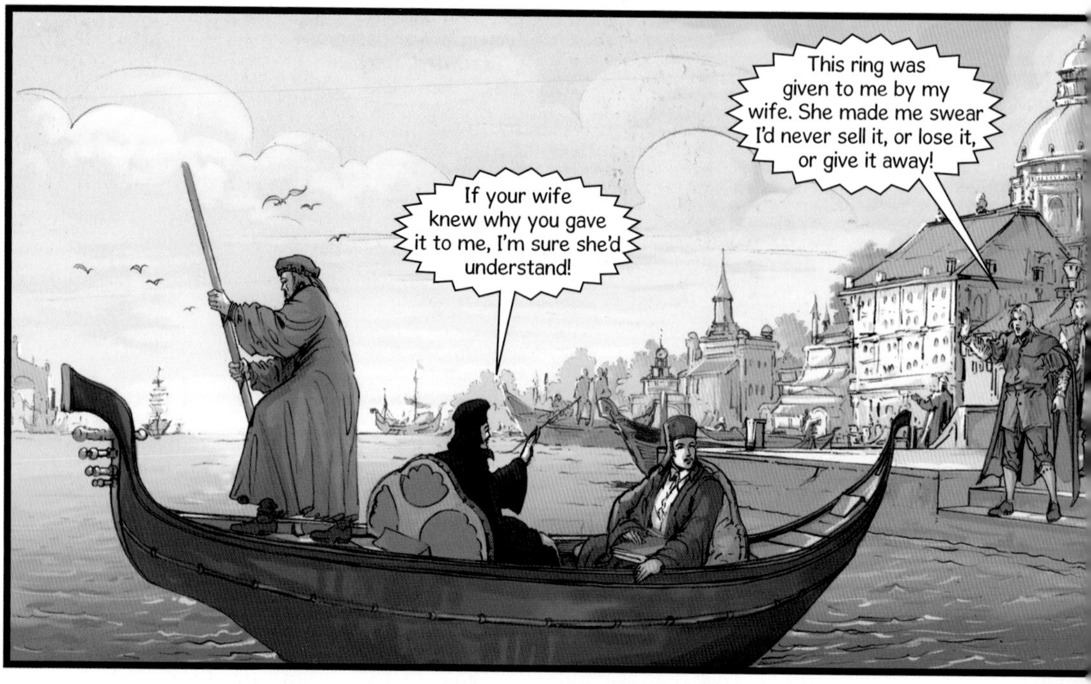
If your wife knew why you gave it to me, I'm sure she'd understand!
This ring was given to me by my wife. She made me swear I'd never sell it, or lose it, or give it away!

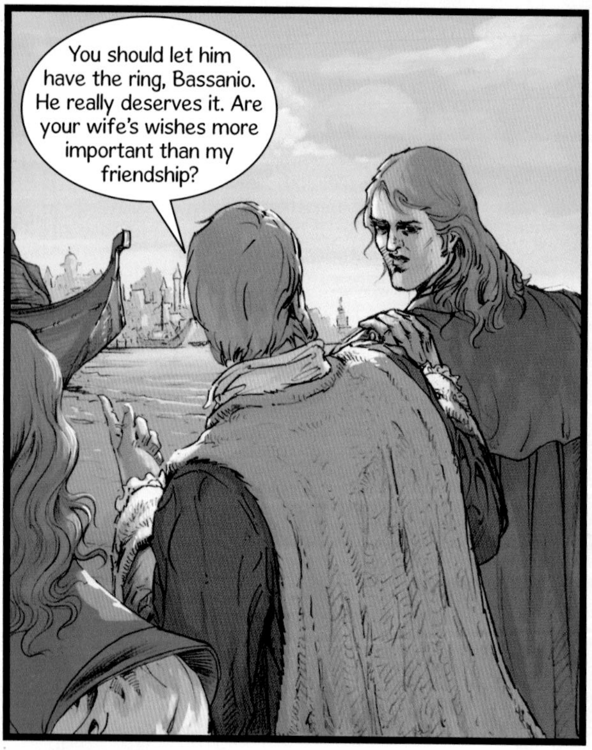
You should let him have the ring, Bassanio. He really deserves it. Are your wife's wishes more important than my friendship?

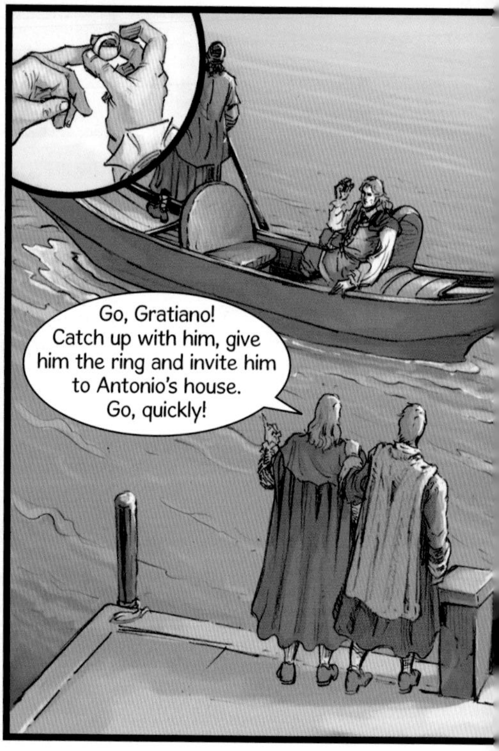
Go, Gratiano! Catch up with him, give him the ring and invite him to Antonio's house. Go, quickly!

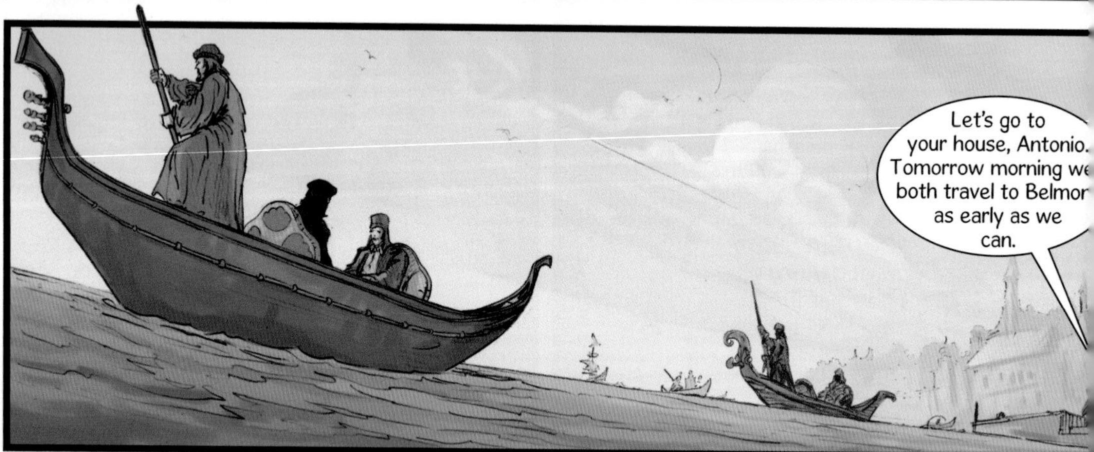
Let's go to your house, Antonio. Tomorrow morning we both travel to Belmor as early as we can.

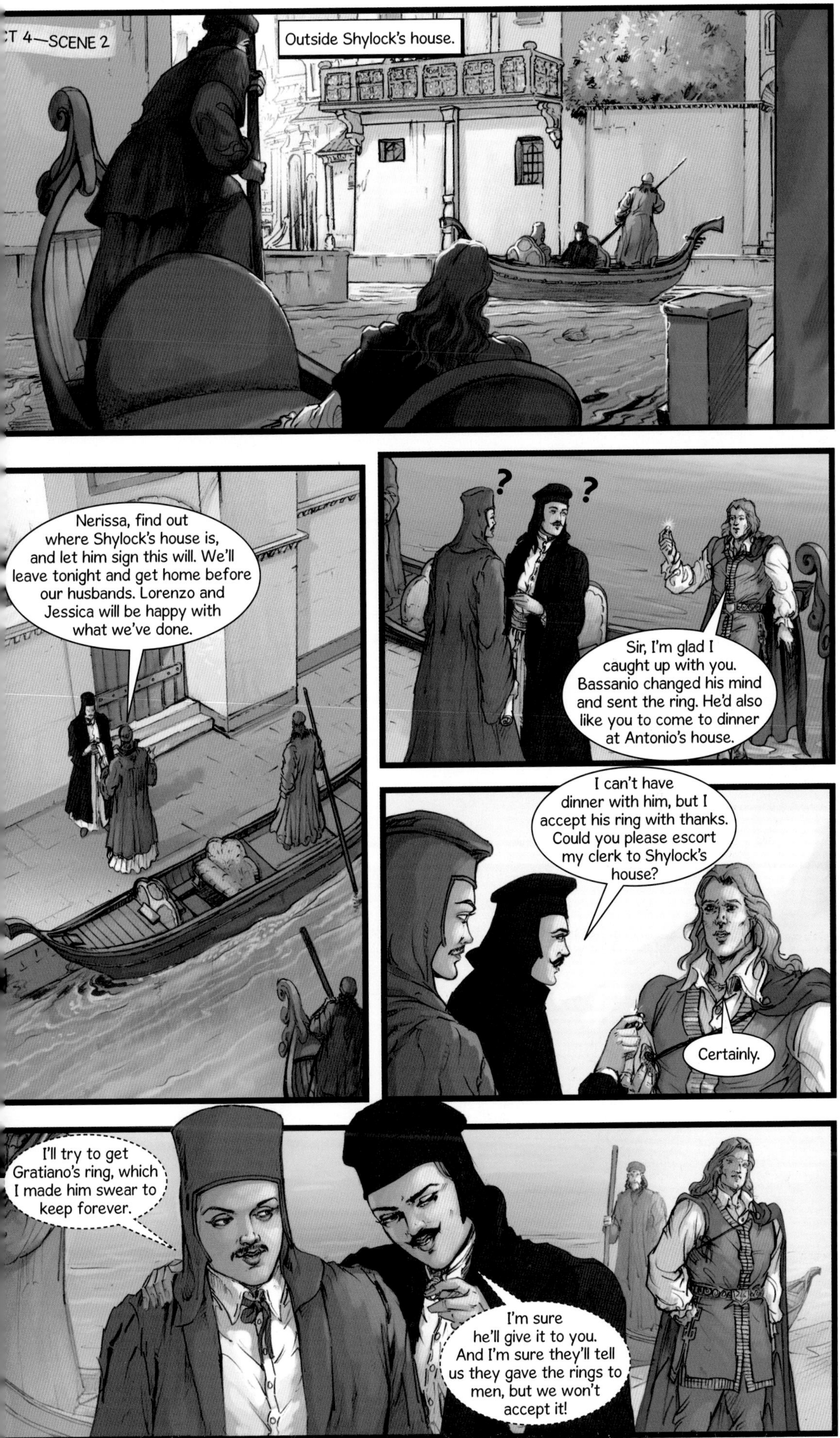

ACT 4—SCENE 2
Outside Shylock's house.
Nerissa, find out where Shylock's house is, and let him sign this will. We'll leave tonight and get home before our husbands. Lorenzo and Jessica will be happy with what we've done.
? ?
Sir, I'm glad I caught up with you. Bassanio changed his mind and sent the ring. He'd also like you to come to dinner at Antonio's house.
I can't have dinner with him, but I accept his ring with thanks. Could you please escort my clerk to Shylock's house?
Certainly.
I'll try to get Gratiano's ring, which I made him swear to keep forever.
I'm sure he'll give it to you. And I'm sure they'll tell us they gave the rings to men, but we won't accept it!

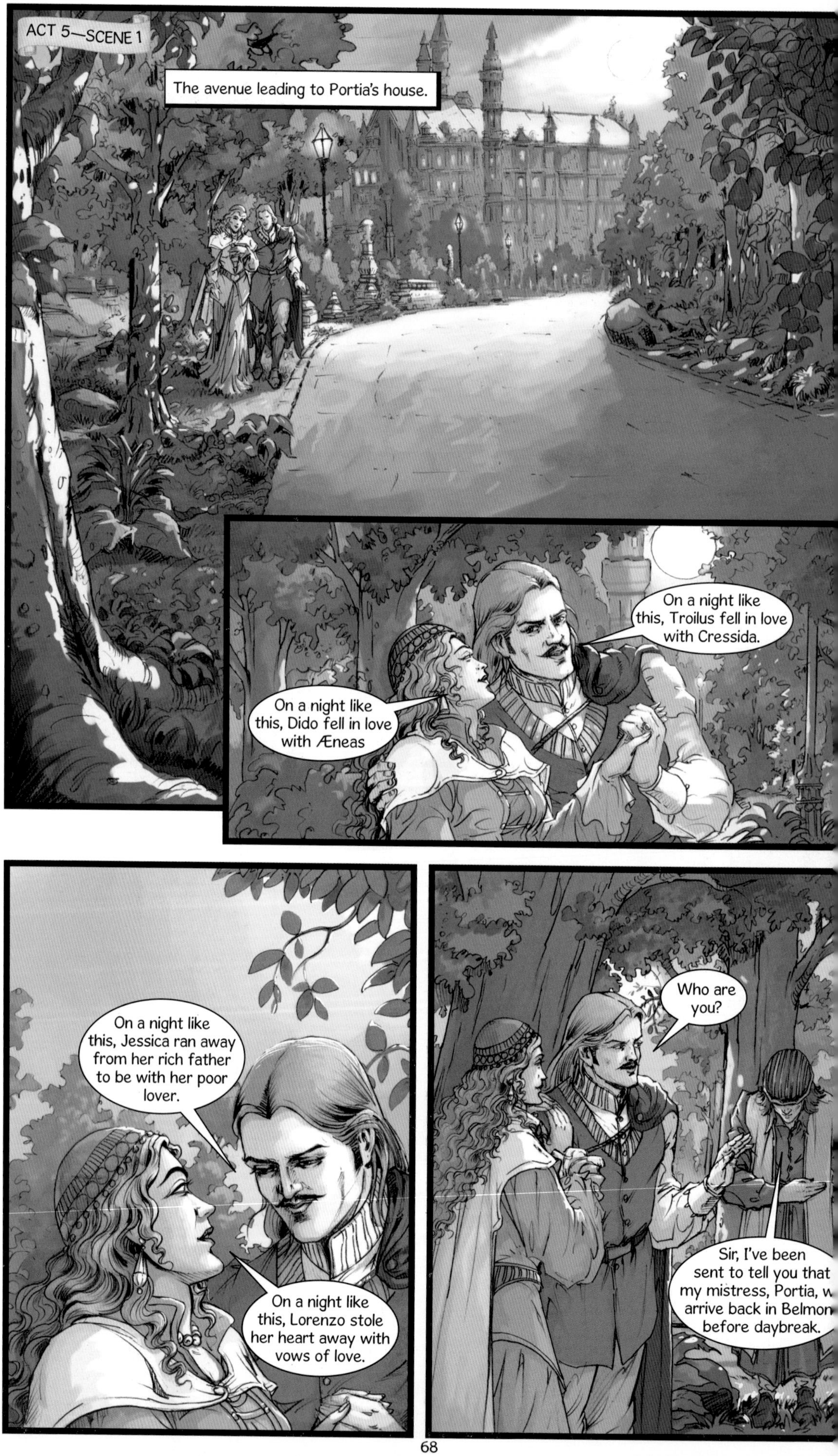
ACT 5—SCENE 1
The avenue leading to Portia's house.
On a night like this, Troilus fell in love with Cressida.
On a night like this, Dido fell in love with Æneas
On a night like this, Jessica ran away from her rich father to be with her poor lover.
On a night like this, Lorenzo stole her heart away with vows of love.
Who are you?
Sir, I've been sent to tell you that my mistress, Portia, w
arrive back in Belmon
before daybreak.

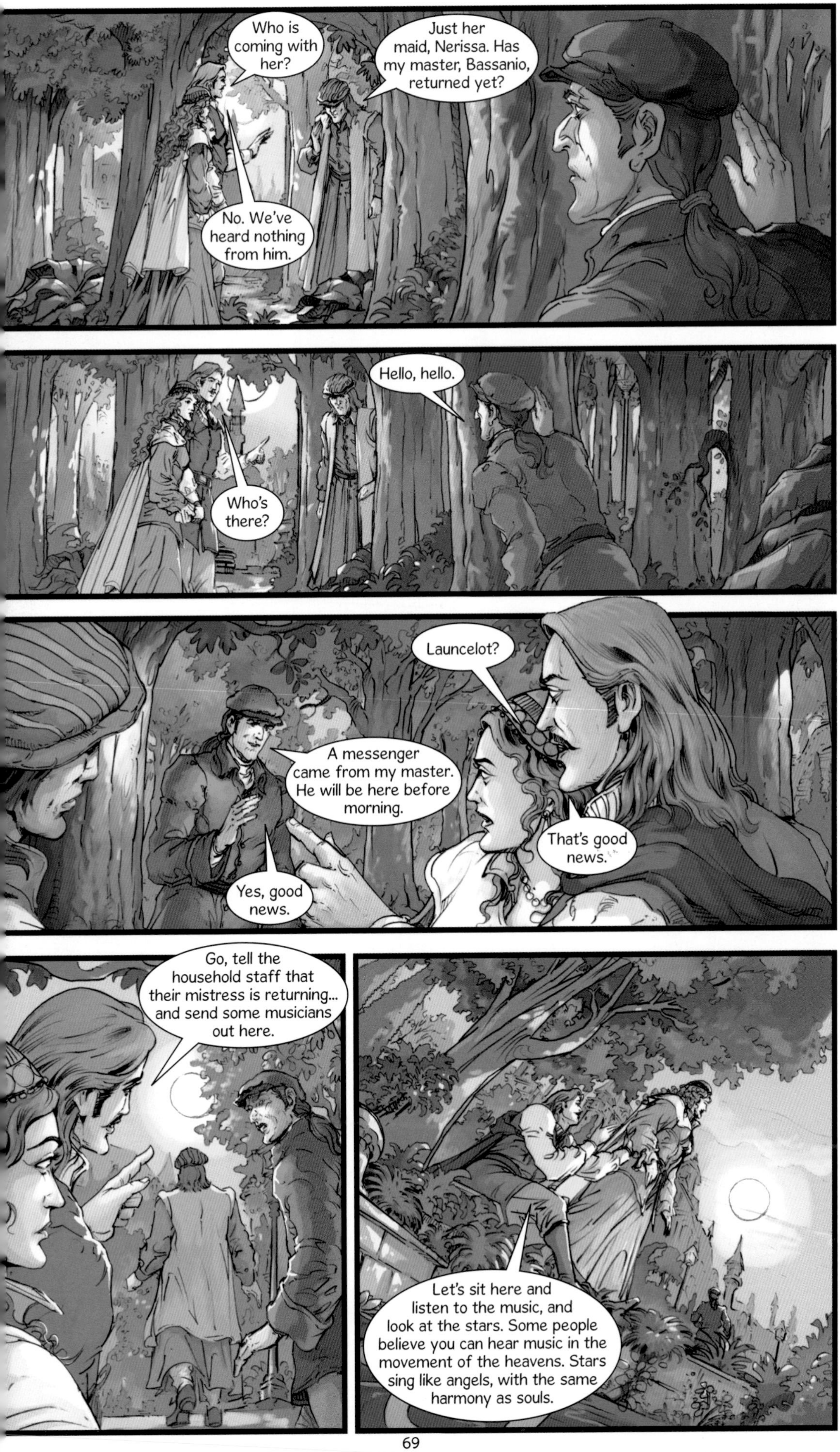
Who is coming with her?
Just her maid, Nerissa. Has my master, Bassanio, returned yet?
No. We've heard nothing from him.
Hello, hello.
Who's there?
Launcelot?
A messenger came from my master. He will be here before morning.
That's good news.
Yes, good news.
Go, tell the household staff that their mistress is returning... and send some musicians out here.
Let's sit here and listen to the music, and look at the stars. Some people believe you can hear music in the movement of the heavens. Stars sing like angels, with the same harmony as souls.

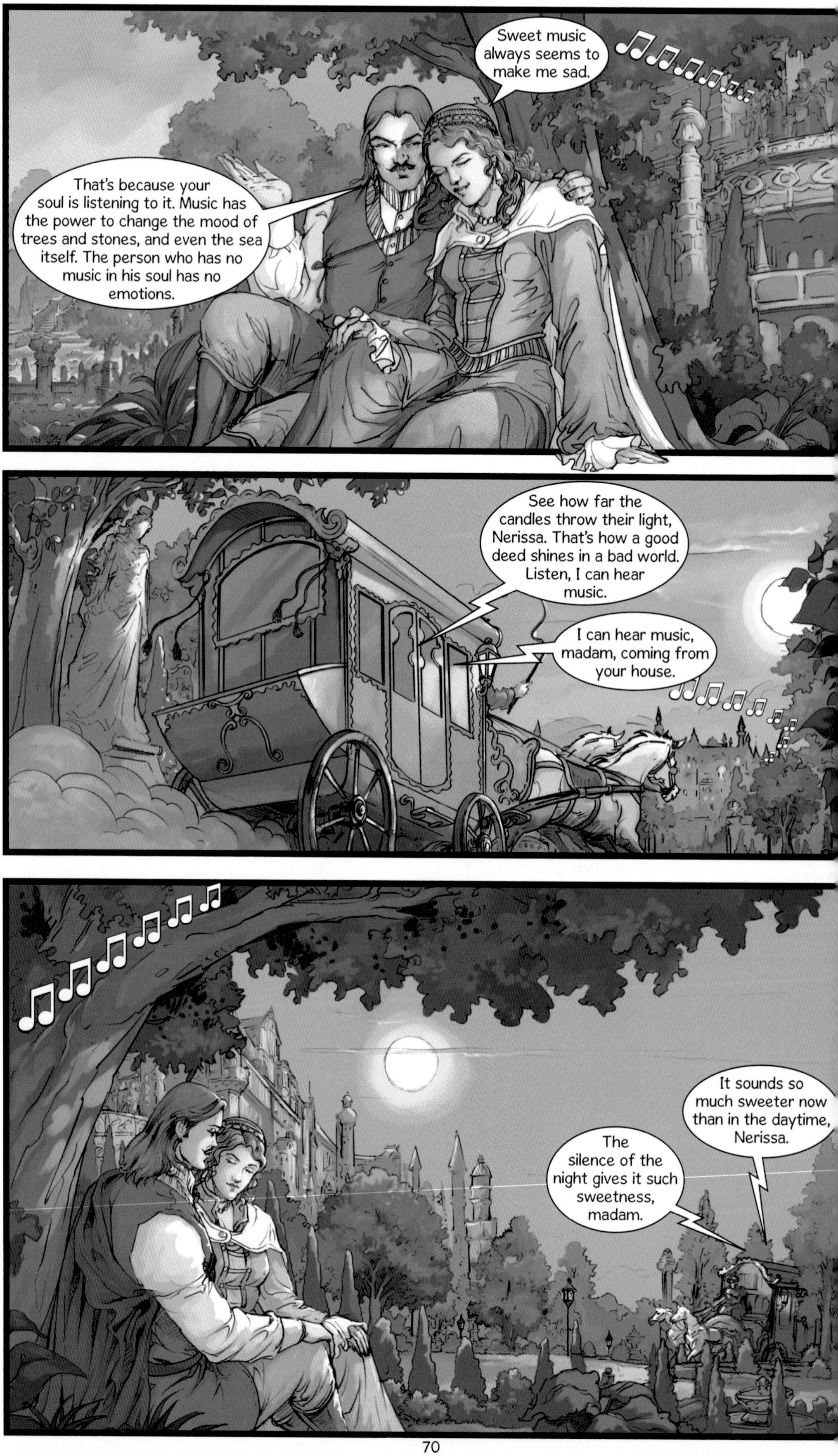
Sweet music always seems to make me sad.
That's because your soul is listening to it. Music has the power to change the mood of trees and stones, and even the sea itself. The person who has no music in his soul has no emotions.
See how far the candles throw their light, Nerissa. That's how a good deed shines in a bad world. Listen, I can hear music.
I can hear music, madam, coming from your house.
It sounds so much sweeter now than in the daytime, Nerissa.
The silence of the night gives it such sweetness, madam.

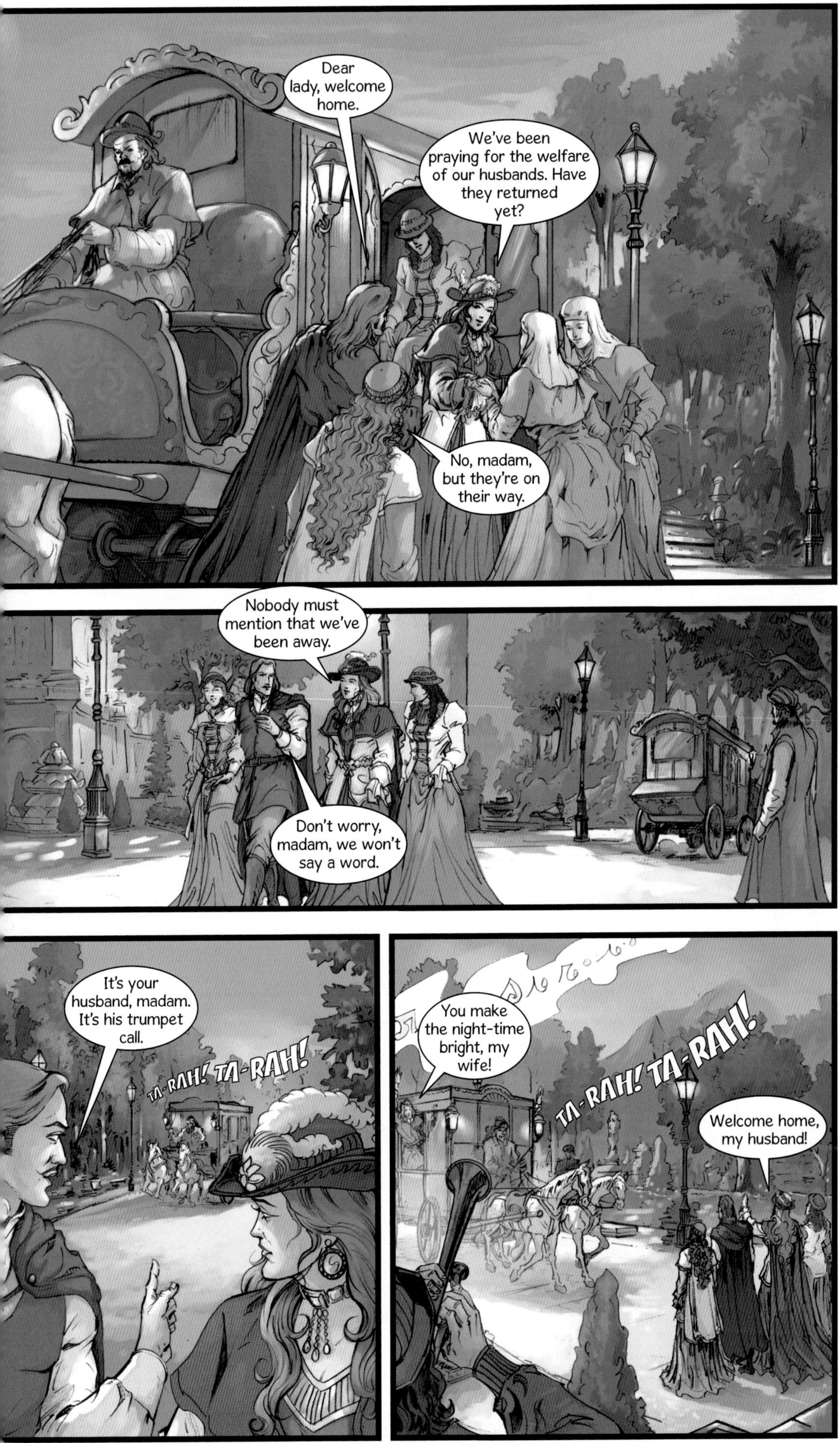
Dear lady, welcome home.
We've been praying for the welfare of our husbands. Have they returned yet?
No, madam, but they're on their way.
Nobody must mention that we've been away.
Don't worry, madam, we won't say a word.
It's your husband, madam. It's his trumpet call.
TA-RAH! TA-RAH!
You make the night-time bright, my wife!
TA-RAH! TA-RAH!
Welcome home, my husband!

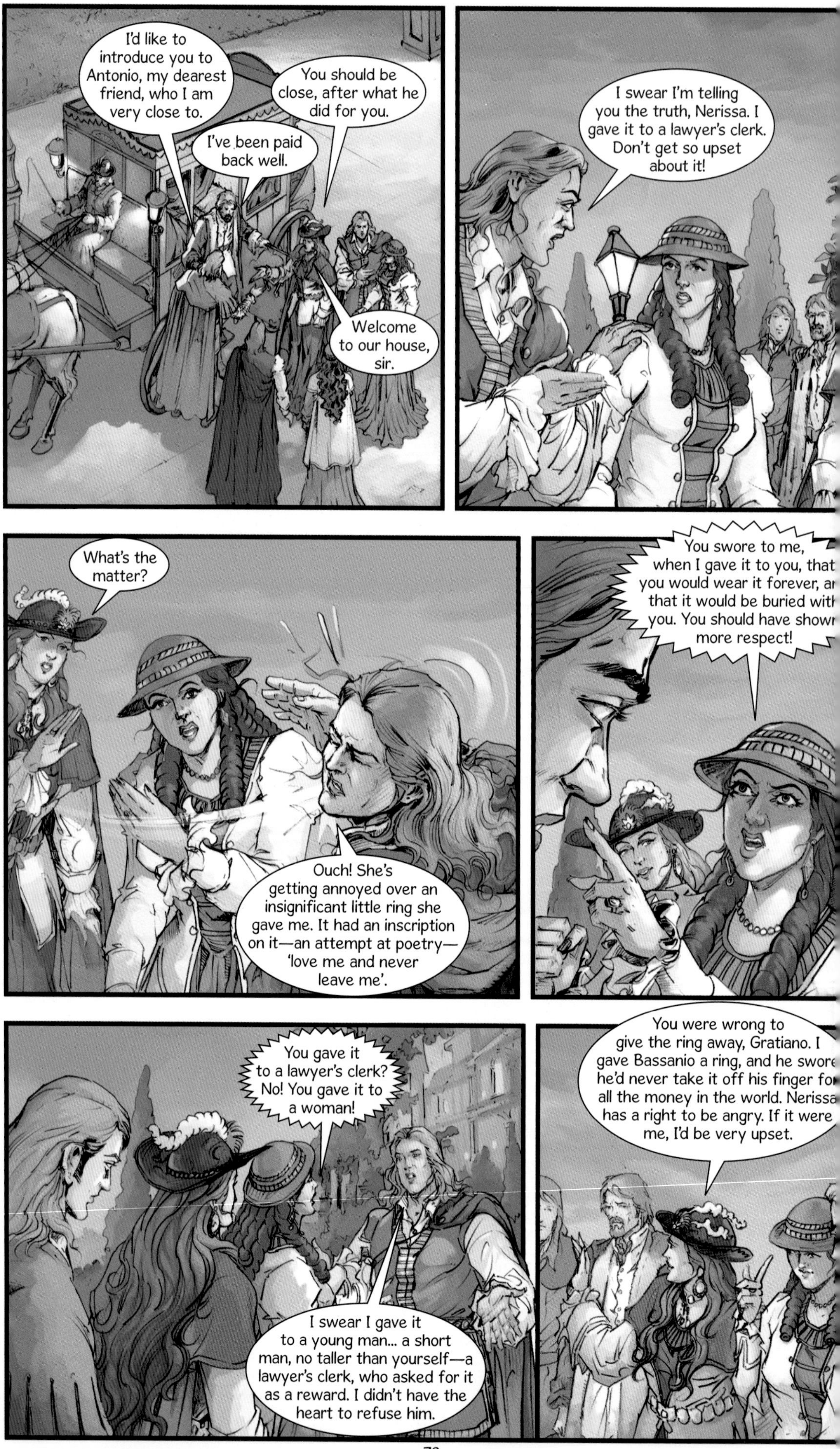
I'd like to introduce you to Antonio, my dearest friend, who I am very close to.
You should be close, after what he did for you.
I've been paid back well.
Welcome to our house, sir.
I swear I'm telling you the truth, Nerissa. I gave it to a lawyer's clerk. Don't get so upset about it!
What's the matter?
Ouch! She's getting annoyed over an insignificant little ring she gave me. It had an inscription on it—an attempt at poetry—'love me and never leave me'.
You swore to me, when I gave it to you, that you would wear it forever, a that it would be buried wit you. You should have show more respect!
You gave it to a lawyer's clerk? No! You gave it to a woman!
I swear I gave it to a young man... a short man, no taller than yourself—a lawyer's clerk, who asked for it as a reward. I didn't have the heart to refuse him.
You were wrong to give the ring away, Gratiano. I gave Bassanio a ring, and he swor he'd never take it off his finger fo all the money in the world. Nerissa has a right to be angry. If it were me, I'd be very upset.

Maybe I should cut off my hand and swear I lost the ring in a fight?

Bassanio gave his ring to the lawyer. The lawyer deserved it too! Then the clerk asked for mine. Neither of them would take anything except the rings.

Which ring did you give away? Not the one I gave you, I hope?

If it would do any good to lie, I would. But you can see for yourself that the ring you gave me is gone.

How can I believe anything you say? I'll never love you again until you get the ring back!

That goes for me too!

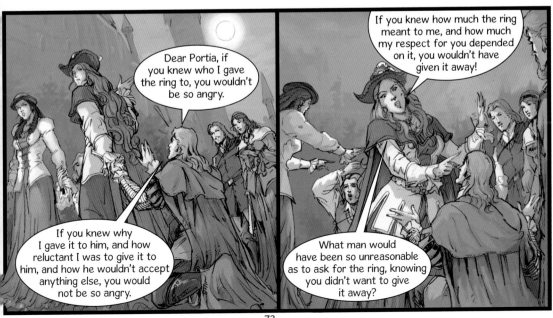

Dear Portia, if you knew who I gave the ring to, you wouldn't be so angry.

If you knew why I gave it to him, and how reluctant I was to give it to him, and how he wouldn't accept anything else, you would not be so angry.

If you knew how much the ring meant to me, and how much my respect for you depended on it, you wouldn't have given it away!

What man would have been so unreasonable as to ask for the ring, knowing you didn't want to give it away?

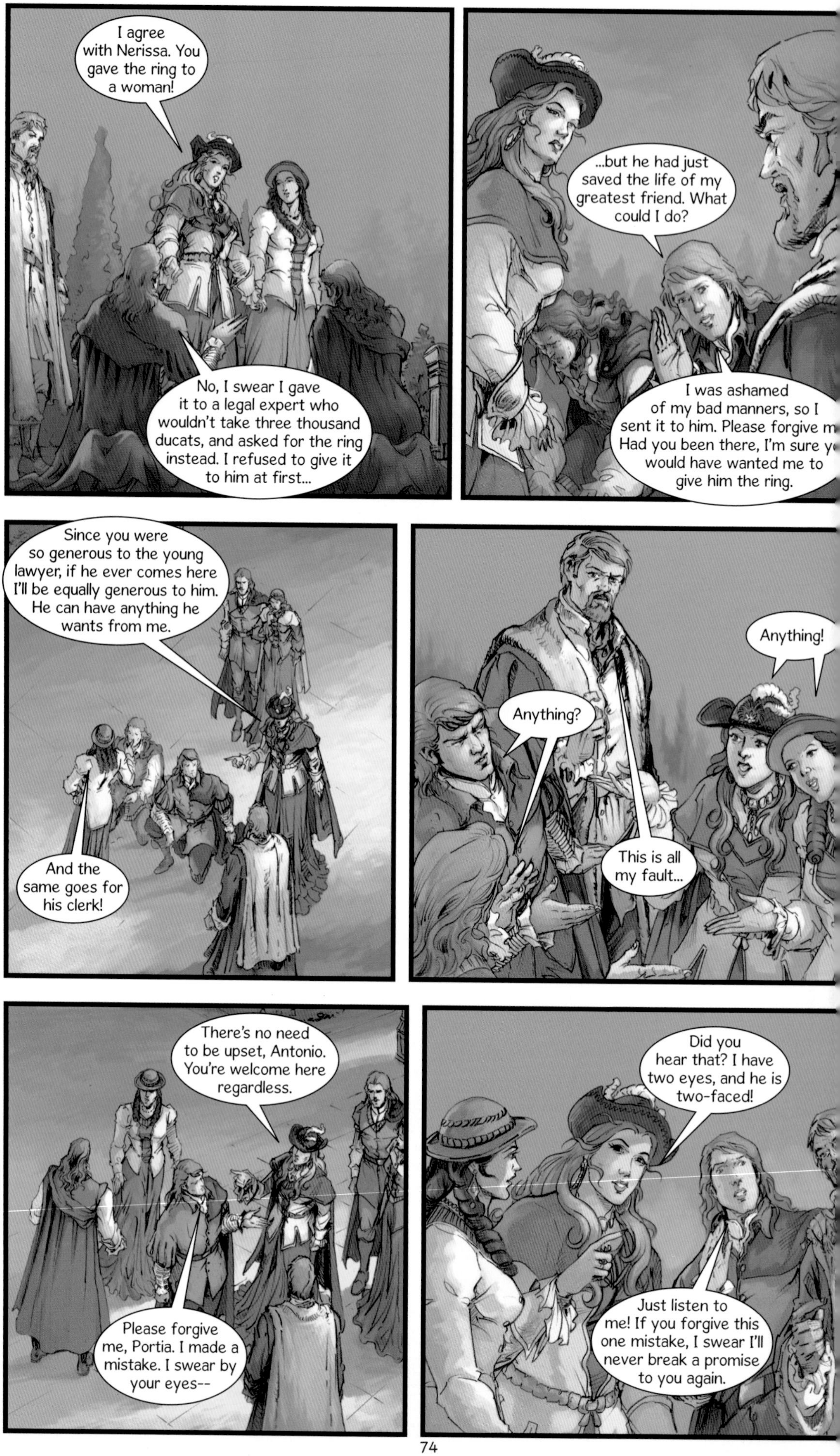
I agree with Nerissa. You gave the ring to a woman!
No, I swear I gave it to a legal expert who wouldn't take three thousand ducats, and asked for the ring instead. I refused to give it to him at first...
...but he had just saved the life of my greatest friend. What could I do?
I was ashamed of my bad manners, so I sent it to him. Please forgive m
Had you been there, I'm sure y
would have wanted me to give him the ring.
Since you were so generous to the young lawyer, if he ever comes here I'll be equally generous to him. He can have anything he wants from me.
And the same goes for his clerk!
Anything?
This is all my fault...
Anything!
There's no need to be upset, Antonio. You're welcome here regardless.
Please forgive me, Portia. I made a mistake. I swear by your eyes--
Did you hear that? I have two eyes, and he is two-faced!
Just listen to me! If you forgive this one mistake, I swear I'll never break a promise to you again.

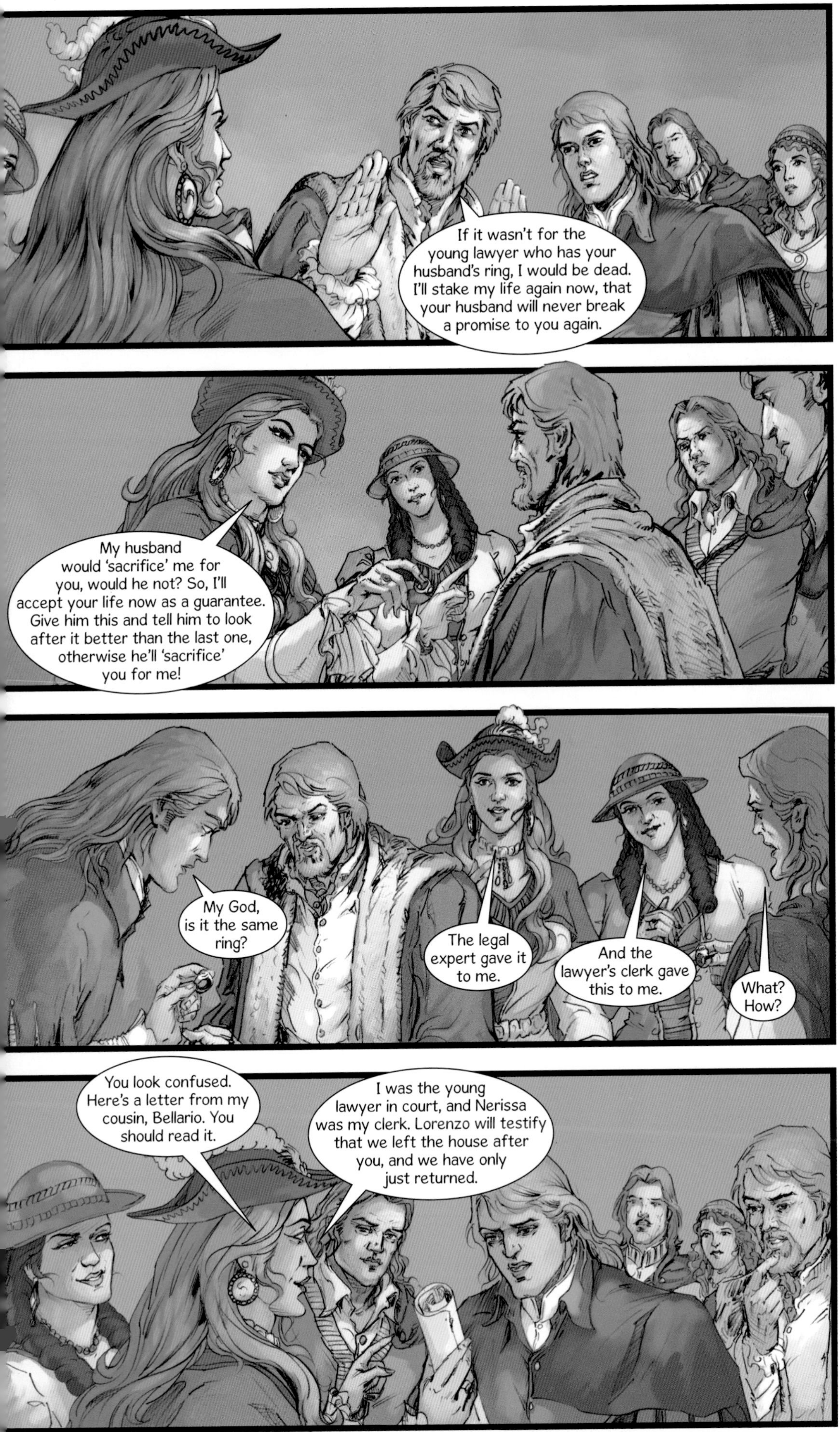
If it wasn't for the young lawyer who has your husband's ring, I would be dead. I'll stake my life again now, that your husband will never break a promise to you again.
My husband would 'sacrifice' me for you, would he not? So, I'll accept your life now as a guarantee. Give him this and tell him to look after it better than the last one, otherwise he'll 'sacrifice' you for me!
My God, is it the same ring?
The legal expert gave it to me.
And the lawyer's clerk gave this to me.
What? How?
You look confused. Here's a letter from my cousin, Bellario. You should read it.
I was the young lawyer in court, and Nerissa was my clerk. Lorenzo will testify that we left the house after you, and we have only just returned.

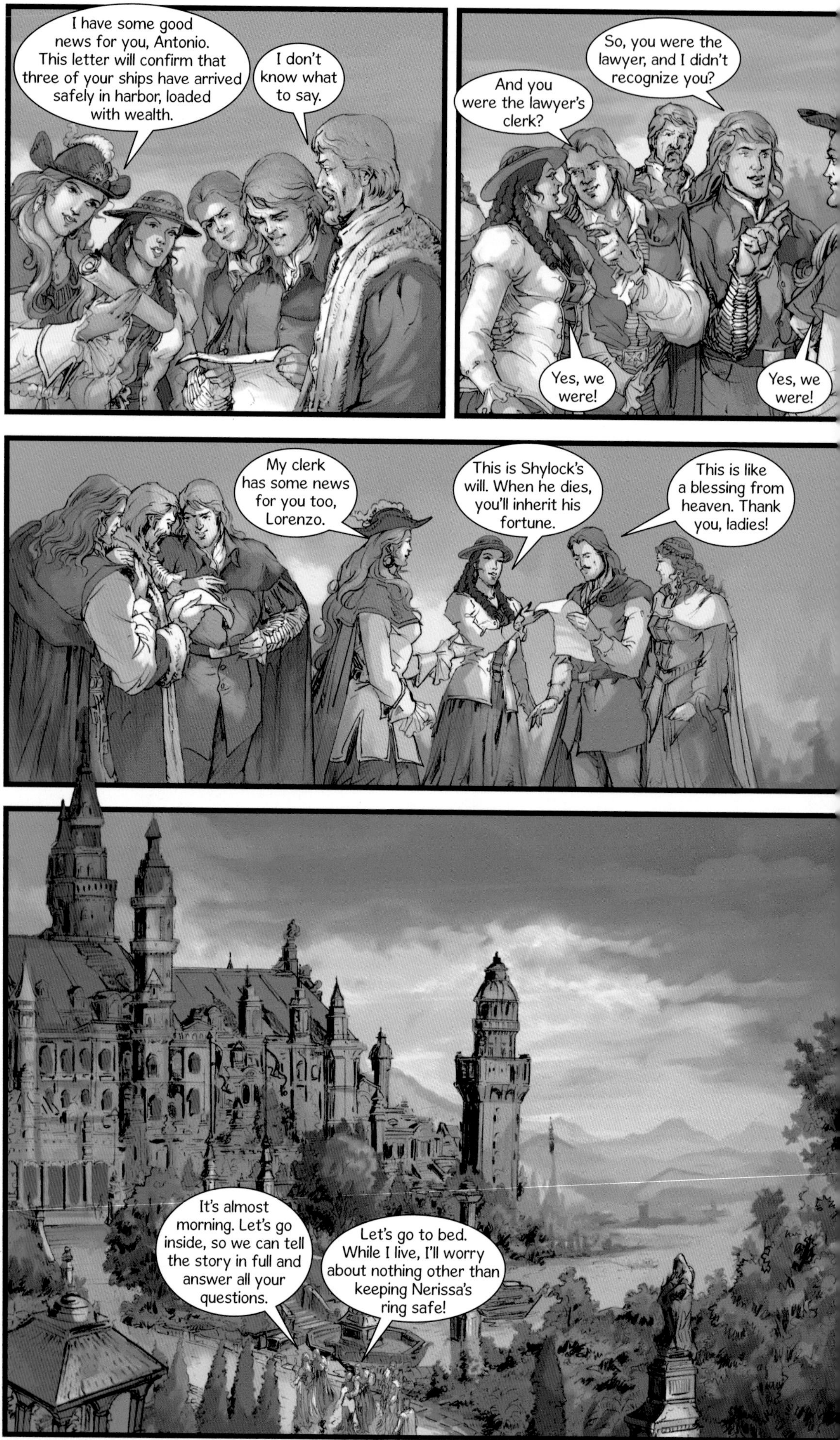

I have some good news for you, Antonio. This letter will confirm that three of your ships have arrived safely in harbor, loaded with wealth.
I don't know what to say.
So, you were the lawyer, and I didn't recognize you?
And you were the lawyer's clerk?
Yes, we were!
Yes, we were!
My clerk has some news for you too, Lorenzo.
This is Shylock's will. When he dies, you'll inherit his fortune.
This is like a blessing from heaven. Thank you, ladies!
It's almost morning. Let's go inside, so we can tell the story in full and answer all your questions.
Let's go to bed. While I live, I'll worry about nothing other than keeping Nerissa's ring safe!

LEWIS HELFAND

400 BC

THE STORY OF THE TEN THOUSAND

Illustrated by Lalit Kumar Sharma

An adventurous tale that throws light on Greek history and warfare.

Fortune favors the bold...

They were an unstoppable force hired to take the crown from the king of Persia. They were a fearless army of Greek soldiers, and one hundred thousand men fighting as one. They were led by the finest and most courageous generals in all of Greece. They were being led to unimaginable wealth, but that was days ago.

Now their leaders are dead and their army has scattered. Their numbers have fallen to ten thousand men and nothing remains but fear. They are men praying not for victory, but for the slim chance of living one more day. Cut off by impassable terrain and pursued by an army of one million enemy soldiers, they must stand together to survive. To find their way home, one of their own must lead them. And to live one more day...

...they must fight.

CAMPFIRE™

Riddles and Giggles!

Many of Shakespeare's plays have riddles that baffle the reader. *The Merchant of Venice* is one of them.

WHAT IS A RIDDLE?

A deliberately mysterious or confusing question that requires a thoughtful and witty answer is called a riddle. It is like a guessing game, and is part of the folklore of many ancient cultures.

ARE YOU A RIDDLE WHIZZ?

Can you solve the riddles below? All you have to do is think out of the box! For every right answer, you get 2 points.

(Answers are at the bottom of the page, but no cheating!)

WHAT AM I?

1. You can hold me without your hands.
2. I cannot be seen but only heard, and will not speak unless I am spoken to.
3. I am an insect, and the first half of my name reveals another insect. A famous musical band had a name similar to mine.
4. I can run but can't walk; I have a mouth but can't talk; I have a bed but never sleep.
5. I've been around for millions of years, but I'm never more than 28 days old.
6. The more you take of me, the more of me you leave behind.
7. I hold all that has been and all that will be; with a device you can see me; when I am short you race me; I am valuable, and once lost I am gone for good.

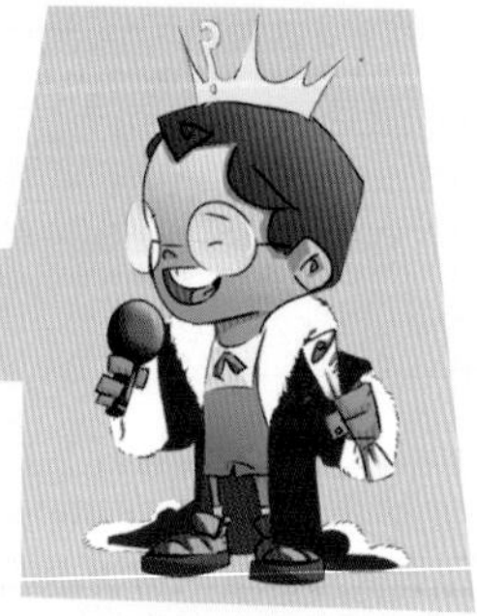

Results

12-14 points: You're a super-duper riddle whizz!

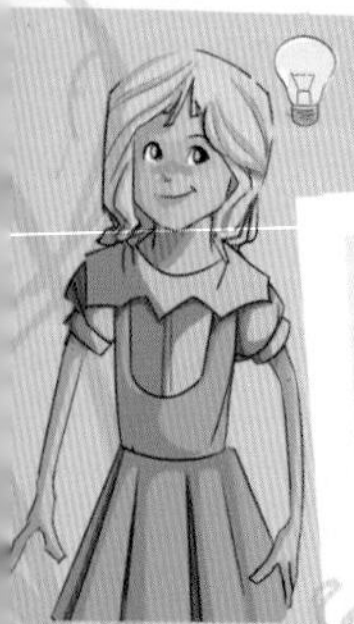

6-10 points: You're good at solving riddles.

2-4 points: We're sure you can be a riddle whizz if you practice solving more riddles.

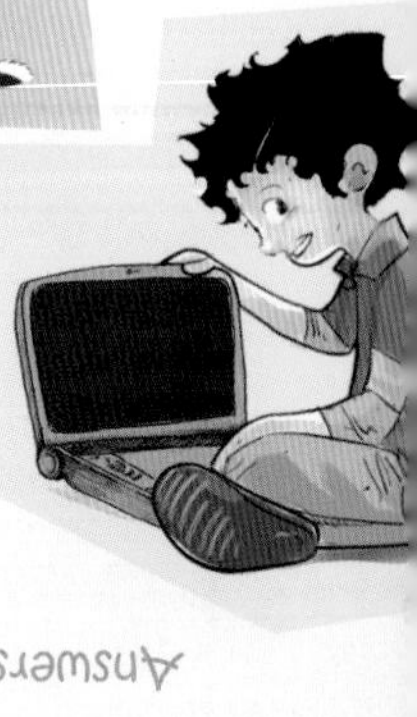

Answers: 1. Breath 2. Echo 3. Beetle 4. River 5. Moon 6. Footsteps 7. Time

Some more tricky ones:

1. What animal's name is 3 letters long, and if you take away the first letter, you have a bigger animal?
2. If you count 20 houses on your right while going to school, and 20 houses on your left while coming home, how many houses have you counted in all?
3. What is yours, but is used more by others?

Answers – 1. Fox 2. 20. You counted the same houses going and coming. 3. Your name

Did you know?

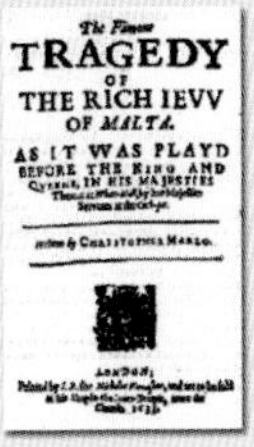

The Famous
TRAGEDY
OF
THE RICH IEVV
OF MALTA.
AS IT WAS PLAYD
BEFORE THE KING AND

- One of planet Uranus's moons is named 'Portia'?
- Shakespeare's main source for the play was *The Jew of Malta* by Christopher Marlow, another successful playwright before Shakespeare? In this play, the main character, Barabas, is hated so much that his enemies boil him in a cauldron!

QUOTABLES FROM *THE MERCHANT OF VENICE*

that glisters is not gold.' These days, however, this quote is more famous as that glitters is not gold'.

at it means is: *Just because something looks attractive, it does not mean that it is genuine or uable.*

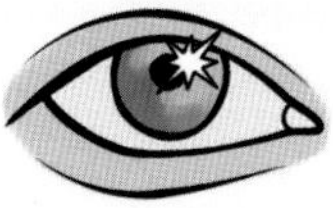

the twinkling of an eye.'

at it means is: *Very quickly*

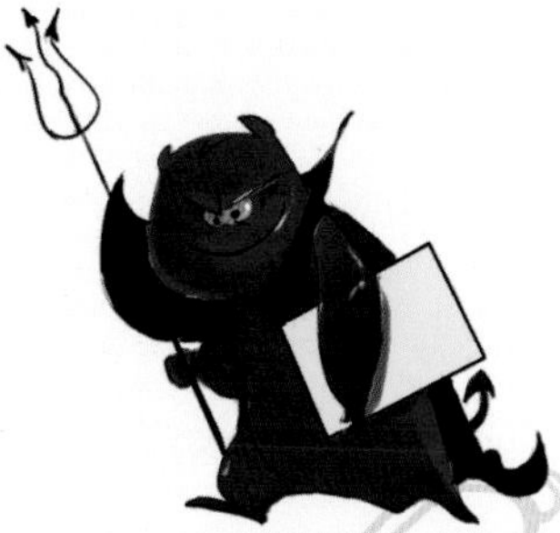

e devil can cite scripture for his purpose.'

at it means is: *Evil people sometimes try to win the confidence of others by saying good things.*